DUNKED IN
TROUBLE

ALLISON PEARL

DUNKED IN TROUBLE by ALLISON PEARL
ANAIAH EDGE
An imprint of ANAIAH PRESS, LLC.
7780 49th ST N. #129
Pinellas Park, FL 33781

First Anaiah Edge print edition October 2019

Edited by Candee Fick
Book Design by Anaiah Press
Cover Design by Laura Heritage

Anaiah
Press
Books that Inspire

For Cyrus, the greatest cat who ever lived
…in my unbiased, completely objective opinion anyway.

ACKNOWLEDGEMENTS

Right off the bat, I'd like to thank Candee Fick, my editor and the unlucky genius who has to see my work "in progress." She rocks, as do all the family and friends who supported Glazed Suspicion. Mom, Missi, Charlotte, Aunt Judy, Sylvia, and Bear, who was probably the first person to buy a copy.
As far as friends go, I've won the lottery. My church family nearly broke my heart with their overwhelming encouragement, which is something no writer can do without. Also, I want to give a special shout out to the girls I used to spend forty hours a week with but now just do bonfires and paint nights with. You guys know who you are. I am so thankful for all the wonderful people God has brought into my life.

CHAPTER 1

THE ONLY THING I WANT this Christmas is a wedding. But how will Nikki feel if her dress isn't the only white in our pictures?

Sheriff's deputy, Josh Bennet, stared out the doughnut shop's front windows at the peace that had been resurrected after the nightmare of the previous weeks. He'd worried the widespread destruction that had nearly cost him and his new fiancée their lives would permanently scar his hometown. But country folks were nothing if not resilient. A few generous helpings of love and hard work had made St. Claire, Pennsylvania better than ever.

The streetlamps flickered on as the sun continued to disappear behind the bare trees covering the rolling hills on the edge of town. The days were growing shorter now.

The grassy isle at the heart of the roundabout looked like his fiancée's chai doughnuts. Dusted with cinnamon from the autumn colors that had erased the last bits of green.

Josh ran a knuckle down the sparkling new panes of cold glass. A few loose shingles on the gazebo in the town center flapped in the wind.

When his gaze shifted to the surrounding bustling stores, he saw Alice Turner struggling against a gust to close the door to Quilting Dee's. A canvas bag spilling over with yarn was in her arms. Josh doubted there was a single person in town who didn't have one of Alice's afghans draped across their sofas. Her long, gray hair whipped over her face as she threw a hip into the stubborn door. She pushed back the strands and pulled her jacket tight as she hurried down the street.

The past few weeks had been unseasonably warm, but today, the weather had grown colder as the hours drew to a close. Would they have snow by morning?

"You giving up on me?"

Josh turned around to find Nikki Appleton smirking at him. She padded across the dining room, the full skirt of her yellow dress brushing the chair rungs as she weaved through the tables.

Look at that beauty. Josh smiled and propped the broom he'd been holding against the seat of a nearby ladder-backed chair. "Never. Just wearing down a bit. I'll get back to it in just a minute."

"Thanks for pitching in so the others could go home. They worked so hard, and they all have to come back tomorrow. Beverly and Roger may be used to the work schedule from before, but they've fallen out of the habit, and Andy's still in school. It was sweet of you to help me close up." Nikki reached a hand behind her head, and a second later, her long, black hair cascaded over her shoulders.

He swallowed and raised a hand to the sudden tightness in his chest. *My, she is stunning.*

"Maybe I just wanted you all to myself." He stepped closer and pushed a wavy lock behind her ear.

Her eyes fluttered close at his touch. "Mmmm. And why's that?"

With the side of his finger, Josh traced the curve of her jaw. "Because it would be the perfect end to the perfect day."

2

Nikki tilted her head to the side. "Perfect but exhausting. I could fill a silo with all the doughnuts I made today."

His eyes fell to a white dusting just above her collar bone. "I can tell. You've got some powdered sugar on you." He dropped his head and swiftly kissed the smudge away. Her breath caught in his ear, and a surge of electricity ran through him.

At last, they were alone. He'd been waiting for this moment since that morning when the grand reopening of Apple's Fritters had been ushered in with one of the greatest words ever spoken. *Yes*. She was going to marry him.

The whole town had been there for the ribbon cutting ceremony after so many had helped out with the repairs. But when Josh had proposed, they'd all had something else to celebrate. Her eyes remained closed as she let out a sigh, and his fell to her lips. He was going to kiss those lips every day for the rest of his life. Starting now…

But Nikki turned away until she was leaning back against him. He wrapped his arms around her, and her head fell back against his shoulder. "I just love it in here. I know it's different from the other shops given that most of those buildings have been there for over a hundred years, but I still can't believe it's mine."

Josh kissed her hair as his eyes wandered around the room. It was true that the shop had changed. The fire had destroyed nearly everything, and they'd had to start over from scratch, but to Josh, her original vision was timeless. Even the folksy flare had returned in the form of the quirky local artists' paintings of doughnuts with cups of coffee that filled the white shiplap walls. "St. Claire is an old town, and I treasure it, but it's kind of nice to have something new."

She lifted her left hand into his view, letting her fingers dance so the diamond twinkled in the soft lighting. "The shop isn't the only thing new."

Seeing that ring on her finger was a dream come true. Did she feel the same? "Do you like it? I wondered if I should let you pick it out yourself, but I wanted to surprise you."

With her other hand, Nikki reached back and touched his cheek. Her delicate fingertips sent thrills down his spine as she continued to gaze at the ring that bonded them together. "It's better than I could've ever imagined."

Josh swept his lips down her neck. "I love you." He slid a hand up her arm and spun her around before taking her face into his hands. Her eyes closed, and she drew in a breath as he leaned in for the kiss he'd been waiting for all day, but the front doorbell jingled. Her eyes popped open, and she twisted away again.

Not another customer.

Pasting a smile on his face, Josh looked up, and his heart stopped as he recognized the newcomer. "What are you doing here?" The marshal should still be in Pittsburgh. Could the investigation be all wrapped up? What about all those unanswered questions?

Nikki smacked Josh on the chest. "Is that any way to greet a friend?" She stepped out of his embrace and walked over to US Marshal, Perry Cole, arms open for a hug.

The marshal leaned down to give her a squeeze, his bright red hair practically glowing next to Nikki's inky mane. "I hear congratulations are in order."

Nikki took a step back and splayed out her hand in front of him. "I know. Isn't it wonderful?"

4

Perry pressed his lips together and adjusted the strap of a leather bag on his shoulder. "Yeah. It's... uh awesome."

Josh narrowed his gaze, and the hairs on his neck stood on end. That didn't sound sincere. Was something up?

"Are you hungry?" Nikki gestured to the kitchen door. "I don't have anything out here, but there's still plenty of doughnuts left in the back. Can I get you something?"

Perry shrugged. "I wouldn't say no to an éclair."

"I'll have it in a jiffy."

Josh waited until he heard the subtle whoosh sound of the swinging kitchen door and then raised an eyebrow. "I'm surprised to see you here."

Perry's eyes darted around the room. "Well, you know, it's a big day for you guys and we've grown pretty close recently." He reached out a hand to tap on the back of one of the dining chairs.

Josh tilted his head. "We have grown close. Close enough for me to sense that you aren't just here to congratulate us."

Perry folded his arms over his chest. A tinge of redness showed under the freckles on his cheeks. "Maybe you should take a seat."

Josh clenched his jaw as he pulled out the chair at a nearby table. "What is it?"

Perry chewed his lip and then took a seat, letting his bag drop to the floor beside him. "I don't think you two can get married right now."

This isn't happening. "And why's that, marshal?"

"Because I've been looking into your former coworker. You know, trying to tie up loose ends. I don't like gaps in my cases."

They still didn't know where the car that tried to run Nikki down had come from, and the rogue deputy hadn't been working alone.

Blood coursed through him. His knee started bouncing under the table. "And?"

Perry pinched the bridge of his nose. "And... I don't think you two are out of danger, my friend."

Josh swallowed. He knew the marshal well enough by now to know when he was scared. "Tell me."

Perry reached a hand into his bag. "I think you'd better take a look at something."

***

Nikki laid a custard-filled éclair on one of the mint green dessert plates Lizzy had bought at an antique store in Pittsburgh. Not only was she about to have a husband, she was also getting a sister. She twirled the ring around her finger. There was no end to her smiling. God's blessings felt endless. For the first time in her life, things were working out. And given how chaotic her life up till now had been, having a place where she belonged felt like a miracle. Nikki glanced through the porthole window in the kitchen door at Josh and Perry sitting at one of the tables. Blood rushed to her face. Would she always swoon at the sight of Josh's broad shoulders and firm body? She pictured her fiancé holding her. The dark skin of his hand wrapped around her pale wrist as he pulls her to him. Her black curls in stark contrast with his thick, golden head of hair.

He'd started the day in his thick, slate sweater, and she'd run her fingers across the high collar the first chance she got, but somewhere in the middle of the thousands of doughnuts and pots of coffee, he'd pulled it off, revealing a black T-shirt that fit snugly against his chest.

Nikki bit at her bottom lip as her eyes moved up the muscles in his arms to his face. But something was wrong. His brow was crinkled, and his fingers drummed the tabletop. Were he and Perry fighting about something?

Only one way to find out. Nikki grabbed the edge of the plate off the counter and tiptoed through the door.

Their voices were low and indecipherable. What were they saying? She squinted at the rushed movements of their mouths, but she was no lip reader. Her eyes fell to the table as she approached. Glossy papers covered it. Pictures. Pictures of her. Her getting into her old truck that had been totaled in the crash. Going into her front door. Buying groceries. Walking down the sidewalk in front of Poppy's Pies and Tarts. Image after image. Why?

"W-Who took those?"

Josh jumped and his gaze swept up to her. "I uh, didn't hear you come back out, babe."

Her stomach churned, and her eyes went back to the chilling images. None of them showed her looking at the photographer meaning… What did that mean?

"Who took them?" Her bones started to quiver.

Perry reached out and cupped his hands under the plate in her hand. "How about I take this so your new dish doesn't get broken?"

The warmth of the glass slid across the tips of her fingers, and she sank down onto the last chair at the little round table.

Perry drug a finger over the chocolate glaze and popped it in his mouth as he stared down at the table. "Since this whole mess started in Pittsburgh, that's where I've been focusing my efforts. When you shake a tree, there's usually more than one bad apple that hits the dirt. I figured maybe I'd get lucky and find the mysterious *monster* you were told about. So, I had a friend of mine in the FBI do some snooping at that Pittsburgh station. He's a bit of an acquired taste, but he's a good agent. Anyway, he looked for friends, colleagues, numbers from old phone records." Perry bit into his éclair and started to chew.

He couldn't wait to eat it until after he gave her some answers?

Perry swallowed. "And, well, it wasn't long until he found that a police officer where our perp used to work went AWOL right after the arrest. It seemed suspicious to me, so I checked out his apartment with my buddy, and these..." He motioned to the snapshots. "These were taped to the wall."

Nikki shuddered in her chair. Josh rested a reassuring hand on her shoulder.

"What do they mean?" Nikki asked Perry as he took another bite.

He shrugged as he chewed and then swallowed, taking a moment to lick his lips before continuing. "I'm not really sure. But I do know your kidnapper wasn't a lone wolf in sheep's clothing. He was part of something bigger. I just can't see how the pieces go together. But... if someone else was watching you, it means you're still dangerous to someone. Nikki... I think you should come into the Marshal's custody and let us hide you until we have more information." The last bit of doughnut disappeared into his mouth.

Josh laced his fingers together on the table, his forearms covering parts of the photos. "How fast can you get her in?"

How fast can you get her in? He was planning to ship her off already?

Grabbing a napkin from the silver holder, Perry wiped his mouth as he finished. "Say the word, and I can take her right now."

Were they serious? "Are either of you planning on asking me what I want to do?"

Perry glanced at Josh.

Josh picked up one of the pictures, holding it up for her to see. "What possible reason would there be for you to stay?"

Nikki folded her arms. "How about the fact that I just got my life back? How about I have a business to run? And—oh yeah—I just got engaged."

Josh shook the picture. "None of those things are going to go away just because you're gone for a while."

Easy for him to say. He hadn't been bounced around foster homes his whole life. How many times had a social worker driven her to a new home and promised she would be safe and that, if she liked it, she could stay, but if it was bad, she could leave? How many times had those words turned into a lie?

Was it about to happen again? One time, she'd been dragged screaming from a respite home that she'd loved. Would she now be ripped from the best life she'd ever had? *I was finally home.*

"I'm not disappearing into some place where everyone is a stranger and I can't even tell people my name." At least not voluntarily.

Perry laid a hand on her arm. "I understand what you are saying."

She shook him off. "No you don't. Neither of you do."

Josh puffed out a breath. "Nikki, this is for the best."

Nikki trusted that he meant what he said, but how could he know that? *He hasn't seen what I've seen.* He was never dropped off at a home packed with sad eyed children he didn't know with all his belongings in a trash bag. He hadn't had to start a new school every few months or sleep in his clothes at night so none of the other kids would steal them. Josh didn't understand all the terrible things that could happen when someone came into your life and said you have to leave everything behind.

"I'm not going."

Josh groaned. "I can't believe we are even talking about this. You're going. Of course, you're going."

Chair legs creaked on the hardwood floors as Perry got to his feet. "I think I'll… uh go wait outside while you two discuss this."

Nikki grabbed the marshal's wrist. "There's no need to wait. There isn't going to be a discussion."

Josh smacked his hand on the table. "Nik—"

"I've made my decision. You don't get to make this choice for me, Josh. And if any part of you thinks you can, we're not ready to walk down any aisles."

CHAPTER 2

JOSH SQUEEZED THE STEERING WHEEL of his sheriff's department cruiser and willed himself to stay awake. He grabbed the thermos in the cupholder and raised it to his lips. He tipped it, but only a few drops of lukewarm coffee trickled out.

He was waiting, lights down and engine off, in the same spot he'd been every night for days. Silent days of unanswered texts and unanswered calls. Josh stared through the trees at the light still on in the top floor bedroom of Nikki's old farmhouse.

Fat raindrops smacked the windshield, filling his ears with white noise. Was it seriously raining? Where was the snow? Predicting the weather in Pennsylvania was always a toss of the dice. Rain in winter? What could they expect next?

The seasons seemed to come and go as they pleased this time of year, and it always made him uneasy. A few hours' time could change the rain to sheets of ice or into a storm strong enough to tear the doors off barns. If he got called out, who would watch her?

If Josh had a choice in this, he'd be seated on the porch, his gun in his lap, ready for action, and not hidden in the brush, but Nikki'd made it clear she didn't want him there. In most cases, her desires would trump his own but not when she had a stalker out there somewhere.

We're not ready to walk down any aisles. The words were branded on his brain. Did she regret saying yes? Had she changed her mind? The wondering was the worst. Of course he didn't think he could make decisions for her. He just wanted to keep her safe. Did she expect him to just stand by and do nothing? Impossible. He wanted to be out there finding her stalker not sitting here all night. Why couldn't she have just gone with Perry? *God, help me find this guy.*

Josh blinked as a shadowy figure dashed across the front of the house.

Maybe the stalker was coming to him. It wasn't like visitors prowling around at midnight were likely to be selling cookies or magazine subscriptions.

Josh grabbed the door handle and elbowed it open. Quick but quiet was the way to go. Determined to keep the element of surprise, he slid through the opening and then used both hands to gently press the door closed as he peered over the hood to make certain the quick flash of the dome light hadn't given away his location. He pulled his service weapon out of his holster as he crept through the grass, being pummeled by the rain.

The shadow lurked at the side of the house heading towards the back. Josh veered left and quickened his pace so he could surprise the intruder on the other side. His footfalls made slurping sounds on the soaked ground, so he shifted his weight onto the balls of his feet and took large, quick steps.

He flattened himself against the old wooden siding and listened for the stranger's approach. A rustling sound and the creak of a foot on the step to Nikki's back porch was Josh's cue to act. He swung around the corner with his pistol pointed., "Stop where you are, and raise your hands. Nadine County Sheriff's department."

"Josh?" The dark figure lifted his palms.

Why was he here? Josh squinted and dropped a hand to his belt to get his flashlight. "Koby? What are you doing?"

Koby turned to face him, blinking in the bright beam. "What do you think, man? You told me to come." He wiggled his hands in the air and raised an eyebrow. "Can I put down my hands now, deputy?"

Josh registered his raised gun, its barrel pointed right at his best friend. *What am I doing?* "Oh, yeah. Of course." He holstered the pistol and snapped it into place.

"You told me you were on graveyard tonight and that I should stop by and check the house for you."

"I got Laney to cover for me." Josh remembered the knowing smile the deputy sheriff had flashed when he asked for the schedule change. "I thought I texted you."

"Yeah, I need to get a new phone." Koby stepped closer. "I dropped it today while I was taking the engine out of an old Ford at my shop. It's on tomorrow's 'to do 'list."

"Ah." Josh nodded. "Thanks for coming."

"...Sure." Koby pulled down the brim of his ball cap against the rain and shuffled on his feet.

What was that about? It wasn't like Koby to be tight-lipped.

"You got something to say?" Josh asked.

"Well… it's been almost a week. Nothing's happened, man. I mean, other than us getting soaked." He stuck his hands in the pockets of his jacket, hunching his shoulders against the downpour. "How long do you plan on keeping this up?"

"Until I know she's safe."

"How can you ever really know that?"

Scratching his stubbly chin, Josh took a slow breath in. How *would* he know? When Heather had gotten sick, he'd felt so useless. When she'd died, a part of him had felt like it was somehow his failure. What if they had gone to the doctor sooner? What if they had taken her headaches more seriously? Would she still be alive? In the end, he couldn't protect Heather. What made him think he could protect Nikki now? "I'm not sure. But I... I just have to do something. This whole mess, I don't think it's over. So, I'm not leaving until it is."

"Is that so?" The angry voice of the woman he loved shattered the moment as the porch light flicked to life and thunder boomed.

Josh's heart skipped a beat. Nikki had a hand on her hip. A glimpse of her shoulder poked out of a baggy, pink sweatshirt dwarfing a pair of gray leggings.

"You guys want to tell me what exactly you are doing here?" She tapped a fuzzy-slipper-covered foot and crossed her arms over her chest.

Josh was nearly soaked through, but her sleep tousled hair made him want to take her in his arms. Josh caught a glint of the diamond engagement ring on her hand. *At least she's still wearing it.* This mess needed to be over. Then they could get back to planning their life together.

Koby shrank out of his periphery. "I'm going to head back through the woods to my ATV. I'll leave it up to Josh to answer that."

"What do you *think* I'm doing here, honey?" He winked, hoping to get a rise out of her. This stalemate needed to end.

A flash of lightning cracked across the sky. "I want to come inside."

She didn't say yes. But… she didn't say no either.

He pulled on the shoulders of his shirt, which was now plastered against his back. How many ways could she leave him out in the cold? "Would you rather just fight out here in the storm?"

"Why are you assuming it's going to be a fight?"

Josh eyed the curve of her neck and remembered kissing powdered sugar off the subtle hollow of her collar bone. His heart started throbbing louder than the rain. "I'm up for some wedding planning if it's on the table."

She rolled her eyes. "Well, you'd better come in before you drown." She went back inside but left the door open for him.

***

Nikki's hands were still trembling as she held her copper tea kettle under the faucet to fill it. She'd been petrified by the voices outside her house being muffled by the wind and rain, but still she'd stashed her kittens in her bedroom and prepared herself for a fight. It had struck her just how much she'd risked by not going with Perry. She'd prayed that God would make her fearless and give her strength. She'd even prayed that Josh would know to come for her.

And then to discover that he was the cause of all that fear? She wanted to kiss him and slap him at the same time.

She turned off the faucet and spun towards the stove. Cold water splashed out of the spout and sent a chill up her arm. She glanced over at Josh standing on the mat at her

15

back door. His hair—normally wavy and thick—was flat on his head, and a little puddle grew around his muddy boots.

She set the kettle on the burner and turned on the gas. "I'll get you a towel." She took a couple steps towards the hall.

"Wait." His voice was dark and desperate, like the beautiful and yet foreboding song of a cello.

Her chest rose as she caught her breath, and his fingers wrapped around her arm. She let him turn her to him but placed a palm on his chest to keep him at a distance. Her eyes locked on the uniform that so often threw him into danger. What if their relationship was just another fantasy she'd never have? She wanted to feel the gray sweater again. Not the sharp edges of his badge and the outline of his gun. Could she just stop being an orphan with a tragic past, and could he stop being the heroic cop that had to keep saving her? Could—just for a moment—they be normal? Could they have a life without danger and secret late night trips?

Icy water dripped down over the ring on her finger. Would this diamond weave their stories together or tear them apart? "You're soaked."

"I don't care."

"You're dripping all over my floor, and this could end up being a long fight."

"I don't want to fight." He stared into her eyes. "I surrender. If you don't want to go into witness protection, you don't have to. I won't argue anymore."

"But you still want me to go." Nikki pulled her arm from his grasp as thunder cracked.

"I want you safe. *Of course,* I want you to go." His voiced trailed her as she hurried down the hall to the bathroom.

16

Did he truly wish she was somewhere else? Her heart clenched as she grabbed a towel and returned to the kitchen. Was he going to be just another family to send her away?

She tossed the towel at his chest. "Can't you see why I won't?"

"I don't know." He blotted his face and arms. "I guess you don't believe there is any danger."

"I'm not stupid, Josh. I know there's danger." Couldn't he see the obvious?

"Then why not go with Perry?" His voice rose.

Nikki hated and loved how she seemed to infuriate her fiancé. "Because... I-I don't want to leave you."

The smooth skin of his brow crinkled. "Leave me?"

"If I went into witness protection, you wouldn't come with me." She caught her breath at the pain that option would bring. *I'd be on my own. Again.* Was catching the bad guy really more important than being together?

Josh's gray eyes dropped to the floor. Proof that she was right.

"It's not that I wouldn't want to—"

"You would stay out in the open until you found every bad guy that could hurt me."

He snorted. "You say that like it's a bad thing. I love you, Nikki. I want to make sure you're safe."

"*And I love you.*" She pushed on his chest and balled his shirt up in her fingers. "And I love my life here. I have my shop and my little country farmhouse and you, so I'm not going to go into hiding while you put yourself in danger without me." She suddenly saw him crumpled on a bed of glass. Blood dripping down his face and arms. She blinked the memory away.

17

"Then I'll come with you." He laid his palm over her fist, squeezing tight. "If that's what it takes, I'll come with you. We'll get Judge Wilcox to marry us in the morning, and then we can disappear together."

Nikki swallowed a gasp. He would really just run away with her? "Y-you would do that? Even though you don't want to?"

"I want *you*." He dropped the towel and pressed up against her. Cupping her face with his hands, he backed her up against the butcher block counter. "God taught us to sacrifice for the people we love. What I want isn't the only thing that's important now. It's not about me. It's about *us*."

He leaned in as if for a kiss and a tingling sensation moved from her toes up to her lips as she let her eyes close. But instead of feeling his mouth on hers, the sound of the screeching kettle stole the moment.

"Ugh." With a sigh, Nikki slid away from Josh's heat so she could stop the steam shooting up like fireworks and dousing her kitchen.

Turning off the burner, she grabbed the handle and turned towards the sink to grab a towel to wipe up the steaming drops. Lightning flashed, and she caught a horrifying glimpse of a hooded figure right outside the small window above her kitchen sink. A scream erupted from her lips, and the kettle slipped from her grasp. It clattered on the tile and shot drops of steaming water onto her slippers and shins. She jumped back out of the line of fire.

Josh bolted out the back door.

"Josh!" What was he thinking? The screen door crashed against the siding and then swung closed only to again be smacked back into the side of the house by the wind. Raindrops flew at her.

She couldn't just stay here and hope he came back. Ignoring the prickles of pain on her shins from the hot water, she raced to jerk open the utility drawer. After pulling out a long, black flashlight, she followed the man she loved out into the storm.

When would he learn that they were in this together? He wanted all the danger and risk on his shoulders even if it meant keeping her out of the loop. *I'm not a child who needs to be spared the truth.* The kid gloves needed to come off.

When she stepped off the porch, the wind hit her like a punch, but the cold water soaking the ground and covering her body felt like heaven on her burns. In her beam of light, she caught a glimpse of a boot rounding the corner of her house. Her slippers sank into the mud, so she pulled her feet free and started running.

When she reached her front yard, she saw a tangle of limbs rolling around in what was now mud. Who was the stranger? She recalled the photos Perry had shown her. Had this man been the eye staring through the lens? She choked up on the flashlight with both hands like a baseball bat. It was the only weapon she had.

"*Josh!*" She charged towards them, ready to jump into the struggle.

Josh glanced her way and let out a growl. "STAY BACK!" The stranger took the opportunity to elbow him in the mouth.

The blow sent him backwards. The attacker was almost free. Where was Josh's gun? Wind whipped her hair across her face, blinding her. She wiped at the wet locks until she could see.

Nikki shone the light across the grass and saw a glint of the black barrel nearby and reached for it. It was smudged with mud and slick with rain. Closing her left fist around the flashlight, she braced it under the grip of the pistol, and then raised the gun, aiming it at the stranger.

He had just wrenched himself loose and was about to make a run for it.

"Don't move! I have a gun!"

His back to her, the man froze and then slowly raised his hands.

Josh rose to his feet and trudged to her, favoring his left side. *Please Lord, don't let him be hurt again.* He held up his mud-covered hands as he reached her and then took the gun from her shaking hand. "I got it." He turned to the intruder. "Who are you?"

"Rob." The voice was low and hoarse.

Josh snorted. "And why are you here, *Rob*?"

The man cleared his throat. "I just wanted to see her."

Nikki clamped a hand over her mouth. *See me?* It was as if a thousand eyes were on her. She was exposed. Violated. Who else was going to invade her privacy?

"Why?"

"To make sure she was safe."

Safe? "Why would you care if I'm safe?" Nikki stepped up to Josh's side.

The man's shoulders slumped in the shaking beam of her light. He twisted his head to look back at her. "Because I'm your brother."

CHAPTER 3

JOSH MAY HAVE PLACED HIS gun down on Nikki's kitchen table, but the barrel still pointed at the guy seated across from him. He could have it up and in the man's face in less than a second. Nikki stood behind Rob, leaning against the counter and picking dirt out of her nails.

His first instinct was that the man was lying. If he was who he said he was, why show up now? What was he planning? A strange man showing up at someone's house in the dead of night was rarely there with good intentions.

Josh shook his head. "Start talking because Ms. Appleton doesn't have a brother. She's an only child."

"How would you know?" Rob smirked through the water and mud running down his face. Josh looked past it trying to find glimpses of Nikki in the man's features.

"Because I told him about why I grew up in foster care. They told me I was an only child and that my parents died in a car accident." Nikki stepped up to the table and sat down, crossing her fingers on the tabletop. "I don't keep secrets anymore."

Rob rolled his eyes. "You have that luxury. You were taken away before you were old enough to remember anything worth hiding. *You* never knew Camille and Andrew for who they really were."

Nikki jerked in her chair. "Andrew and Camille Appleton are the names of my parents."

21

"The names of *our* parents." Rob tilted his head at Josh and narrowed his gaze.

"Why should we believe anything you're saying?" Josh recalled the panic in Nikki's eyes outside, as well as the glimmer of hope that she might not be alone in the world. Except, she had him. "What proof do you have?"

Rob glared at him and then shook out his hand, sending mud and water to the floor and reached into his jacket.

"*Easy.*" Josh laid a hand on his weapon.

"Relax, officer. You already patted me down outside. It's just a picture. I promise I won't hit you with it."

Josh's chin burned where Rob had elbowed him, but the heat was more than pain. It was anger. But if he picked a fight with Rob, he risked picking one with his fiancée too. Next time he and Rob clashed, though, things would be different. Josh nodded and the man pulled out what looked like an old photograph and tossed it on the table. It slid under the gun and lodged between the grip and the tabletop.

Josh tilted his head to mirror the sideways image. It was old. The corners were creased, and the white frame had yellowed with time. The picture was of a couple with two young children. One child, a girl, who couldn't have been more than two or three, but the little boy looked six or seven. The whole group was bundled up in winter clothes, and snow topped the trees behind them. All appearances indicated a happy, little family playing outside on a wintery day, red cheeked and grinning.

The boy *could* be the man sitting across from him. They both had dark hair and large eyes, but it wasn't definitive. His skin was fair like Nikki's, but while her eyes were clear and blue, Rob's were dark. Josh squinted at the picture. The boys eyes weren't blue, but Josh couldn't identify the shade. The color seemed to have faded over time.

He couldn't see much of his fiancée in the little girl either, but the resemblance was clear as day in the mother. Josh wasn't quite sure yet who this Rob was, but the woman in his picture was definitely Nikki's mom.

Nikki took the photograph into her fingers like it was glass about to shatter.

Josh kept silent, laying his hand over her arm, prepared to give her all the time she needed, but suddenly red and blue lights flashed outside the windows. Grabbing his gun and Nikki's hand, Josh rushed towards the front window, throwing open the drapes to the sight of black SUVs filling the lawn.

He'd seen these vehicles before. Josh glanced over his shoulder at the mantel clock sitting on the bookshelf pressed against the back wall of the den. It was the middle of the night. Why would the US Marshals be there now?

"What do they want?" Nikki wrapped a palm around the bend of his elbow.

"If I had to bet, I'd say him." Josh twisted around and looked down the hall into the kitchen, but Nikki's maybe-brother was gone.

The back door swung open on its hinges, and a path of muddy water led out into the storm. Coward. Josh stepped down the hall, but the hand on his arm tightened. He glanced at Nikki. Her wide eyes looked pleading. The pain in his jaw urged him towards retribution, but he couldn't leave her like that. If the marshals wanted Rob, they could find him themselves. His concern was his future wife. She

23

shivered, still wet with rain and mud. Josh holstered his gun and wrapped her in his arms.

Three loud knocks pounded on the door. "It's the marshals! Open up!"

Josh released Nikki and crossed to the door to open it. Perry stood on the front porch with two of his agents a step behind. "I'm assuming you're here for our guest."

"What guest?"

"Rob Appleton." He had to spit out the words, then swallowed back the sour taste they left on his tongue.

Perry pushed past them into the hall, leaving behind muddy footprints right alongside Nikki's and his own. She cringed as he passed, her eyes on her hardwood floor. His future home was becoming quite the wreck.

"He's here?!"

So I guess Rob wasn't lying. Josh's stomach churned.

"Not anymore." Josh shrugged. "He just bolted."

Spinning around, the agent barked orders to search the area.

It looked as though his so-called friend was keeping secrets. After all, how did Perry know Rob and why would he keep the man's existence a secret from his sister? Josh had a sinking feeling that he and Nikki had just been pulled into someone else's dangerous mess.

Perry turned back to face them. "Get back inside."

"You don't need my help looking for him?" Josh raised an eyebrow. Was the marshal deliberately trying to keep him out of the loop?

"We need to stay with her."

Was she in danger? Josh reached an arm across Nikki's waist to push her behind him. She didn't budge. But rather ran her hand down his arm and pushed it back to his side. "Why? I thought you were here for Rob."

Perry grabbed his lapels and shook his blazer, sending water droplets onto the hall floor. "His presence was just a happy accident I'm afraid. I'm actually here for you." He pointed a finger at Nikki.

"*Me?*"

Josh draped an arm across her shoulders and pulled her close. Would Perry try and take her? Josh laid his other hand over the snap of his holster. His fiancée wasn't going anywhere without a fight.

Perry stretched his neck from shoulder to shoulder. "Listen, can we sit down or something? I've been up all night and this… well, it might take a while."

Josh glared at him. "Talk first."

Perry huffed but then threw up his hands in mock surrender. "Have it your way, man. I got word from Robert Appleton's contact at the agency that he had disappeared from WITSEC, and I feared the worst. I rushed here to make sure whoever got him didn't get you too."

Disappeared? WITSEC? Rob was in witness protection? Josh frowned.

"Wait…" Nikki stepped forward, shaking off Josh's arm as she raised her hands to her face. "My brother was in witness protection?" She pushed her fingers into her temples and moved backwards as if she was thinking of making a run for the back door. For her brother. Then her face, twisted in confusion, morphed before his eyes. She pointed a finger at the marshal. "*You knew!*"

***

What a disaster. Rain, mud, and a kettle of spilled water had been tracked all over the downstairs floor. The cotton head of the mop in Nikki's hand hit the tile with a thud. Forcefully, she pulled it over the brown pools covering her kitchen floor. She couldn't wait to get into something dry but the mud and water all over her tile and newly stained hardwood *had* to be cleaned up.

Josh's fingers ran down the middle of her back. "Why don't you let me do that, honey?"

She jerked away from his touch. "I can do it myself. I want you two to go sit on the front porch before you dirty *every* room in my home. I will come outside when I am ready to talk to you."

Josh's jaw dropped. "I don't know why you are mad at me. He's the one who lied to you."

"It was for her own good, and I didn't lie." Perry insisted from the kitchen doorway. "I just didn't tell her."

Nikki turned from her stress-cleaning and shot him a glare she hoped was as menacing and murderous as she intended it to be.

Perry shrank back a step into the hallway. "Okay, okay. We're leaving. Come on, deputy." He flicked his hand, motioning for Josh to follow.

Josh frowned and rocked back and forth on his feet for few moments before glancing up at her. His eyes practically screamed the words 'we need to talk.' He had a point, but, right now, she was in no mood to finish the fight that had started this crazy night. She averted her gaze as she chewed her bottom lip, and at last she heard footsteps, clear evidence that he'd followed Perry into the hall.

When she heard the front door close, Nikki let the mop fall out of her hand as she sank onto a chair. Tears filled her eyes and bubbled over her lids as she retrieved the worn photo Rob has left on the antique white tabletop, still damp from the dish cloth she'd run over it before she started mopping. The edges were smudged with mud now, but it didn't dampen the smiles in the frame. What a happy family. Yet, she couldn't remember them at all. Looking at her mother was like looking in the mirror, but the woman was a stranger to her all the same. What kind of child forgot their mother? Rob hadn't forgotten. He'd come for her. She wanted to stare at those faces all night and will herself to remember something, anything, about them. But when she let the picture fall into her palm, she felt the rough edge of paper on her skin.

Flipping the image over, she saw a torn corner of ink-filled paper taped to the back. Instantly, she recognized the purple, floral print, and her eyes darted to her old refrigerator. The top sheet of the magnetic notepad she kept on the scuffed door to keep her grocery list had a piece missing from the bottom. And not only that, the tape dispenser that was usually in a cat mug on her kitchen counter sat on her table just a few inches away.

There was no doubt about who left the breadcrumbs for her to follow. *My brother* she said to herself, trying to get familiar with the concept. Carefully, so as not to tear the paper, she slid her nail under the tape and separated the scrap. A single message was scrawled hurriedly on the blank space. It was short and to the point. *Don't trust the deputy.*

CHAPTER 4

JOSH'S EYES SWEPT OVER THE four chairs gathered around the little table, stopping at Perry seated in the one next to his. *How is he so calm?* Josh couldn't seem to stop his knee from bouncing up and down, and the wind sent chills up his body, but the marshal didn't seem bothered at all as he rocked back and forth in a slow, consistent rhythm. "You want to fill me in, or are we just going to sit here and freeze?"

"Your girlfriend will be out here eventually. I don't feel like telling the story twice." Perry let his head fall back, and his eyes flutter closed.

"Fiancée." Josh wrapped his arms around his chest. He should've taken the towel Nikki'd offered him when he first dripped all over her kitchen. But he hadn't been thinking about the cold then, just the blush in her cheeks when he pulled her close.

"Fiancée." Perry echoed. "Last time I was around you two, it didn't end well. I didn't want to be presumptuous."

Josh was about to insist the marshal start talking when he caught movement out of the corner of his eye. A bulletproof-vest-wearing marshal stepped over the stairs and onto the porch.

"Sir?" The agent narrowed his gaze like he was wondering if his commanding officer had fallen asleep.

"Yes," Perry didn't bother to open his eyes.

28

"We lost Rob. We've got trails everywhere. From the deputy's car to the back of the house. From the woods to the house. From the house to the woods. We've even got a mud pit out front pooling with rain that you obviously took a dip in." The agent motioned to Josh. "But it all stops at the tree line. Two sets of prints disappear into the woods out back. We tried to follow but lost them in the woods."

Perry's eyes popped open. "Do you think someone was with him?"

Josh held out a hand. "I can explain the second set of prints. I had a friend here checking on the place. He would've went home that way since the trails make it a faster route than the roads. He said he parked his ATV a ways out."

Perry gripped the arm rests of his chair and pulled himself forward before looking at Josh. "Could your friend have seen him?"

Josh shrugged. "He might have, but I can't call and ask. His phone is broken. He owns Koby's Auto Shop about ten miles east of here."

Perry twisted in his seat and held a finger up at the agent. "Get someone over there to see if he saw anything. And then update Rob's agent, Neal Boggs, so he can start a search of his own. After that, form a perimeter around the property. I want this place locked down until we figure out our next move."

"Yes, sir." The agent did an about face and jogged down the stairs.

"That's a lot of protection from just one man." Josh raised an eyebrow. There was no way this is all for one escaped witness. Perry had already admitted to hiding his knowledge of Nikki's brother. What else could he be hiding? And how much danger would his secret put Nikki in? "Do I need to be worried?"

"You're in law enforcement, Josh. You should always be worried."

Josh refused to accept that. Life was hard and bad things did happen—a lesson learned all too well on the battlefield and later when his wife Heather had passed away—but Josh trusted that God could weave His plan for him and Nikki into even the darkest of circumstances.

The porch light flicked on, and then the front door popped open and Nikki emerged, carrying a tray with a pot, teacups, and all the stuff needed for making a hot cup of tea. Some towels were thrown over her arm, and two blankets were wedged between her elbow and hip.

Josh jumped out of his chair. "Can I help you with that?"

Her gaze stayed on the steaming pot. "I got it."

"I'll… uh at least close the door." He crossed behind her and pressed the door closed before turning back and retaking his seat.

The porcelain quivered as she placed the tray on the little glass and wrought iron table in the center of the gathered chairs. She handed them each a blanket and towel. "I thought some tea would warm you up."

Josh laid the towel over his hands and buried his face in the terrycloth. Then he dabbed the it down his arms and chest. He glanced over at Perry, but the man was already digging through the labeled tea sachets, the towel slung over the back of his chair. *How is he not as miserable as me?* Then again, Perry just walked from his SUV to Nikki's front door while Josh had run around the house and gone swimming in a mud puddle.

Josh shook his head and turned back to Nikki, taking the opportunity to observe his future wife. She had changed out of her wet clothes. A dark, baggy sweatshirt and jeans buried her curvy figure. Her anger seemed to have dissipated, but Josh caught the hint of something else in her eyes. The hunch in her shoulders in the glow of the porch light cast a shadow over her body that stretched down to her feet. Doubt and uncertainty seemed to lay in the slight bend of her shoulders and the way she pushed her wavy black hair behind her ears. It made him uneasy. But why?

Leaning back against the porch rail, she crossed her arms over her chest.

Josh motioned to the chair to his left around the little table. "Don't you want to sit down?"

"I'm fine."

She didn't even look at him. Rain was dripping over the porch roof like falling pebbles, and some of it had to be hitting her. Was she purposely keeping distance between them? Would she rather get rained on than be close to him?

Her eyes locked on Perry. "So…"

The marshal straightened in his chair. "So."

"I have a brother."

Josh hoped the sudden stab of jealousy that he was no longer the only man in her life didn't show in his face.

"Yes."

Josh squeezed his hands. Was he going to have to shake the story out of Perry? Out with it already.

"How long have you known?" The ends of her hair were flipping in the wind.

Perry tipped the spout of the kettle over his teacup and filled it to the brim before offering the kettle to Josh. He waved it away. He couldn't just sit there making tea during this mess.

"Since I first came down looking for your fugitive ex. I think maybe you should sit down for the rest of this."

"I'm fine standing," she said through gritted teeth. "Why didn't you tell me I had a family?"

"Because, if you recall, I thought you might be a criminal at the time."

Flashing lights from one of the SUVs backing away from the porch lit up her glare with red. Josh winced at the recollection of how bad Nikki had been treated while under police suspicion.

She bristled. "But when you found out I was innocent, you still didn't tell me."

"I'm not allowed to reveal the location or even the *existence* of people in WITSEC. I couldn't put him in danger."

Josh didn't buy it. He knew the sound of a company policy.

With a note of snark in her voice, she imitated him. *"Couldn't put him in danger? Really? From his sister? Do you know how long I've wanted to have a family?"*

Josh swallowed, slightly hurt that she didn't yet realize he was her family. He passed the towel over his face once more but couldn't wipe away the sting of her words.

"I'm not saying you would hurt him. But someone could have used you to hurt him. If the wrong people found out he was alive, they could use you to lure him out of hiding." He looked down into his cup like he was mulling something over. "In fact, that's exactly what I think happened."

That was plausible. *It could easily happen to me.* If Nikki's life was in danger, he'd do anything to save her. Were his suspicions of Rob misplaced? It seemed that he'd shown up in the middle of the night uninvited for the same reasons Josh had. To keep her safe.

"Tell me." Nikki ordered.

The marshal took a sip of his tea. "When you were little, too little to remember, your parents were killed in a car wreck that was not an accident." He pushed out a breath through gathered lips. "Your parents weren't exactly law-abiding citizens. But… I'll get to that later. Anyway, you were at daycare. They were on the way to pick you up but were run off the road, and their car caught fire."

Nikki held a hand over her mouth. Her eyes went wide.

Perry rocked forward setting down his teacup. "I-I'm sorry. I didn't mean to upset you. The report said you knew about the accident."

Josh rose to his feet and took a step towards her, but she waved him off. "I'm fine. I did know about the accident, just not about the fire. Just… just picturing it. I'm fine, though." She turned back to Perry. "What happened next?"

Josh sank back into his chair.

"Listen, maybe we should stop. I shouldn't even be telling you half of this."

Seriously? Josh spun in his chair and pointed a finger at Perry. "No. You are not clamming up on us now. She deserves to know about her family. So no more company lines about your hands being tied. This isn't about protecting the reputation of your agency. This is about protecting Nikki. We want the truth. The *whole* truth."

Perry's head fell back against his chair, and his gaze rose to the white-stained panels of the porch roof. He seemed to be mulling things over.

Nikki shifted against the railing, the side of her mouth curling into a half smile as if she could sense the scales tipping in their favor. "Perry, please."

The marshal let out a sigh, and his chin fell to his chest. "Your brother—he was only seven at the time—freed himself before the paramedics made it to the scene. It was a miracle he survived. He had broken bones and a burn down his back that would scar him for the rest of his life…" Perry paused, eyeing Nikki warily. "Your parents, however, didn't make it out. The marshal's office used the wreck as a cover story to make Rob disappear. The lead investigators had Rob's death reported to the local news and then transferred him to WITSEC. He knew details about your parents criminal activities and the dangerous people they were associated with. Details that could get him killed. He was placed with a family."

"And Nikki *wasn't*?" They just left her abandoned? Josh squeezed his fists.

Perry pulled together the skin of his brow. "From what I can tell, it was decided you were too young to remember anything that could have put you in danger, and the marshals didn't feel it warranted putting you in the program. I don't know all the details. It could've been that the cost of the monitoring, provision, and protection was more than they thought necessary, or—"

"So, the marshals just left me to be raised in foster care without my only family because it was expensive?" Nikki seethed, her hot breaths puffing into the cold air.

Josh grunted. What they did to her was wrong. "Unbelieve. This is how a federal agency handles protection?"

Perry flinched. "Hey, I wasn't the agent on her case and had nothing to do with how that played out. This was way before my time. But think about it for a minute here. If you'd been reunited with your brother, you'd eventually have learned who you really were, and that would be risky. Rob's knowledge never led to any arrests because he didn't know any names. They showed him mug shots for the better part of a year seeing if he recognized anyone and came up dry. However, as long as the criminals were still out there, Rob was still in danger. As for you..." he pointed to Nikki. "It could've been a what-you-don't-know-can't-hurt-you kind of thing. They could've been trying to keep you out of danger."

Nikki smacked a hand on her thigh. "And I wasn't in danger in foster care? Do you know what my life was like there?"

Perry sank down in his chair, folding over on himself a little. "I have no excuses for that. The lead investigator documented that you should be tracked sporadically, but beyond that, it was blank. When your ex was charged with murder and your association with him was made public, it sent a flag up at the marshal's office, and they discovered the gap in monitoring. However, they didn't just sweep their mistake under the rug but did what they could to help you out."

Josh got a sinking feeling. Would the lies ever stop?

35

Nikki's eyes went wide with suspicion and disbelief. "How did they help me out?" She pressed her hands to her stomach.

Perry cleared his throat. "You didn't actually have an aunt that left you the money that you brought here to St. Claire to start your shop. That was the marshal's office's attempt to rectify what they had done."

Nikki pushed herself off the rail and started pacing. "So many lies! My whole life was just someone else's lie."

"It was for your protection." Perry pleaded. "If *they* would have—"

Josh had heard enough. Anxiety throbbed in his chest. No more stalling. No more skirting around the core issue. "Who are *they*? Your bosses messed up her life, and you still haven't even told us why. Who did Rob see that was so dangerous? Who wants her brother dead?"

***

"It's not *they*. It's *he*. At least, we think it's a he."

Nikki felt the last of her energy draining away with the weakening rain as she paced over the creaking boards. A foreboding shiver tickled across her skin, and she gave into the marshal's earlier suggestion to sit. She stopped between the two empty chairs, then sank into a seat, choosing to sit by Perry instead of near Josh. She saw a glint of confusion and hurt pass over Josh's face. Why had she done that? What had changed? Did she really believe that the message from her brother was about Josh?

Don't trust the deputy. After she'd read it, she'd told herself it was nothing. Only God held more of her trust than her fiancé. He'd saved her life over and over again. Especially from the other deputy that she'd been foolish enough to trust. Was it possible her brother had somehow heard about that? Was that where his suspicions of Josh came from?

Then again, Josh had also helped her find the faith that had transformed her life. That made her feel like a whole person. Why would he have done that if he meant her harm? If she had no doubts about his love and devotion, why had she passed him over? She grabbed her armrests, ready to push herself up and fix her mistake.

"He's called the Snitch." Perry's voice jerked Nikki from her thoughts. She leaned back.

"The Snitch?" Josh scoffed. His mouth twisted like Perry was just jerking their chain.

The agent nodded and picked up his teacup, draining the last of it. "But don't think the cops don't hate him as much as other criminals do. The Snitch is a friend to no one."

"Why?" Josh stared at Perry. His full detective mode expression was tight and inscrutable, as he leaned forward and propped his elbows on his knees.

"He's a counterfeiter. Currency, mostly, but pretty much anything else if he gets the itch. Apparently, he's the best the treasury department has ever seen."

"You'd think that would make him a legend among his peers, not a pariah." Josh rolled his eyes.

"Well," Perry looked past her, leaning to the side to look around her like he was making sure all his men were out of ear shot. "It's what he does with the money that puts him on every hit list from here to California. Using small time drug dealers, he buys up large amounts of drugs with the phony bills, essentially trading a bunch of worthless paper for hundreds of thousands of top quality merchandise. Then, his minions sell it to other suppliers themselves for genuine cash."

Josh tipped his head like he was impressed. "Now, I can see why they hate him."

Nikki grabbed the part of her sweatshirt laying over her heart. "That sounds like a choice that leads to a short life. How is he even still alive?"

Perry tilted his head and flicked a hand. "Because no one knows who he is. He's mobile. Goes from city to city recruiting two-bit dealers while still somehow keeping his identity secret from them. They do the actual deals and get a cut, and then he moves on before anyone is the wiser. Most suppliers don't realize the money's fake and put it back into circulation, leading to their arrests once it's traced back to them. We think that's how the moniker 'Snitch' started. Because he's getting his fellow criminals arrested. But don't think the cops like him either. Sure, they're getting the accidental fallout of arrests for counterfeiting and drug trafficking, but it's minor league compared to what the Snitch is getting away with. This guy's got a lot of blood on his hands." Perry leaned forward, simmering as red blotches climbed up his neck. "He doesn't care what happens to the small-time dealers he's using. You can't imagine how risky it is for the dealers he's using for the initial purchases. Once rumors about the Snitch eventually got around, some of the suppliers started checking the cash at the time of sale. And you can guess what happens to the Snitch's pawns when their money comes up phony."

"Why would anyone gamble with their lives to help him?" Josh wiped a hand across his forehead. His face twisted like he was nauseated.

"It doesn't appear that they know they're walking in with funny money any more than they know who they are working for. The suppliers just kill the small-time dealers over the bad cash and move on to the next transaction. Although sometimes, they torture them for information they don't have before they do."

"My goodness. How cruel." Nikki cringed. Pure Evil. Her stomach churned at the image of criminals abusing and murdering each other all because of this man's fraud and lies. Was an evil like that what had kept her from knowing the only family she had?

Perry puffed out a breath and stretched out his arms and back, like he was trying to calm himself. "He takes years off at a time, too, so he drops off the radar. He's been running this game for decades. Somehow, he's hiring his dealers and suppliers without revealing anything about himself that would lead either the cops or the criminals his way."

"Well, you've certainly proved your point. This Snitch is a scary guy, but what does this have to do with me and my family?"

Perry swallowed hard and dropped his voice. "Your parents knew who he is. And it's possible your brother does too."

CHAPTER 5

JOSH PRESSED HIS FINGERS AGAINST the tension headache growing above his left eye as Perry tromped down the porch steps to talk to his team, leaving him and Nikki alone. "Do you believe him?" Josh asked.

"I do." Nikki's voice was as tight as the arms wrapped around her like a shield against the cold or maybe... him. Should he go to her? An hour ago, he wouldn't have asked himself a question like that. Why shouldn't he touch her? Comfort her? Things had changed between them somehow. *Why?* He pulled his blanket from the back of his chair and got up, holding it out to her as he sat down in the chair next to her. She let it hang suspended between them for a second but then pulled it onto her lap.

"I do, too. I know he's lied to you, but, as impossible as it sounds, I think he's laid everything on the table now. He wouldn't risk telling us intimate details of the case just to hold back other ones."

She looked past him as if trying to read something in the black of night. "So my parents and this Snitch guy worked together a long time ago counterfeiting art. But then he went off on his own and started making money and stuff. Years later, my mom and dad find out the horrible things their old partner is up to and decide to identify him to the FBI. But before they can meet, the Snitch kills them?" She shook her head. "Stuff like this only happens in movies."

"But why would he come clean about the marshals office screwup only to keep more secrets?"

"I don't know." She pulled on a lock of her hair. A habit that usually sent his heart fluttering with affection but now triggered anxiety. She was coming to conclusions. Were they about him? Would he like them? *Lord, let her see the truth in me.*

"I guess I just don't understand why my parents didn't just drop a note in the mail to the FBI saying, 'The Snitch is this guy!' instead of orchestrating to meet them in some clandestine-spy-movie sort of way."

Josh knew why. That part of the story was the least surprising to him. "The FBI gets thousands of letters with crazy tips like that. They wouldn't have taken it seriously. At least, not before a bunch more people died. Your parents probably knew that the FBI would want proof, which would mean revealing their own…" He winced. Why remind her? He should've figured out something else to say.

Nikki narrowed her gaze. "Their own what?"

"Nik—"

"Just say it. Or do you want to keep things from me too?"

Josh groaned. "Their own criminal activities. Chances are, they wanted to arrange some kind of immunity deal that would include all of you being placed in witness protection." Josh rubbed his hand on the armrest of his rocking chair. "The Snitch… he just got to them before all the pieces were in place."

"I don't know what to think about this anymore." She bit at her lip as if trying to stop the trembling in her chin. "Having a family is all I ever wanted. It's why I stayed with

41

my ex-boyfriend in spite of how he treated me. He was all I had. But now, to find out that my parents were criminals? How am I supposed to feel about that? I don't know who I am." She pulled the blanket up under her chin and leaned her head back against the chair.

Josh's heart broke for her. He'd never known what it was like to feel so alone. He reached out a hand and squeezed her shoulder. Tears glistened in her eyes.

Josh always had close family and friends, and he knew how much of a support they were. Honestly, he didn't think he would have survived Heather's death if not for his parents and his sister, Lizzy. She was already a big city lawyer by then, but she had dropped everything and come home when Heather got sick. A couple times at the hospital, Josh had walked in on Lizzy praying over Heather as she slept. Praying that God would comfort her and strengthen him. A support system was more precious than gold, and for years, Nikki had only had foster family after foster family.

Nikki sniffed as she straightened in her chair, the movement knocking his hand away.

No wonder trust was hard for her. The only constant Nikki had had in her life had been her abusive and controlling ex. True, that man had tried his best to protect her at the end before being killed himself, but the terrible things he had done to her would always live on in her memories.

"You feel how you feel. There are no wrong emotions here." Josh sighed and looked out into the yard. The lights had stopped flashing. The marshals most likely didn't want to give away their position. But the monstrous black shadows the SUVs made stuck out like a sore thumb.

"What about anger?"

Josh looked over at her. Her lips were flattened, and there was a hard look in her eyes. "It would be weird if you *didn't* get angry at your parents."

"I don't think it's them I'm mad at."

Josh leaned towards her chair, drawing his knees towards her. "Then who?"

She rubbed her hand up her face and into her hair. "I feel like I'm the one I should be angry at. That I'm the one who's done something wrong."

Just like before, she was taking on others' guilt. "Why would you possibly feel that way?"

"Because something must be wrong with me, Josh. Every person I love has turned out to be bad news."

"I'm not bad." Josh reached out a hand, wanting to brush his fingers against her cheek. "And you love *me*."

She backed away from his touch, and Josh swore he saw a glimpse of what looked like accusation in her eyes. "Nikki, what's wrong?"

Her lips parted. Their life—that happy picture of a wedding, of a family—was slipping through his fingers. *Am I losing her?* Josh steeled himself for the answer. Whatever it may be.

"We need to talk about the plan for tonight." Perry interrupted, jogging back up the wooden stairs.

The marshal's timing couldn't have been worse. Josh tried to hold his fiancée's gaze, but she broke away, her shoulders relaxing as if glad for the interruption. What couldn't she tell him?

"I'll let you guys talk." Nikki gathered the dishes on the tray. "I'm going to go inside."

Perry waited until the screen door shut behind her. "I'm going to run into town and get set up at the Inn. I've got some calls to make, but I will be back to check in. Rob's agent will be down here from Detroit as soon as he can, but apparently Rob left a fake trail that took him so far out that the term wild goose chase doesn't do it justice." The marshal's lips curled into a smile.

Josh rolled his neck. His muscles were stiff just like his uniform under the dried mud. He wanted to jump in a shower and let the heat erase the lingering effects of his tussle with Rob. "Why would he lead his agent away? Why abandon his protection?"

"Hard to say." Perry tried and failed to hold back a yawn. "But from what I've been told, Rob Appleton, is one smart cookie. Like a crazy high IQ or something. He wouldn't have done it for no reason."

Josh snorted. Rob definitely had a smart *attitude* but Josh couldn't attest to any genius level deductions behind all that sarcasm. "What was this about a plan you wanted to discuss?"

Perry nodded. "Right. I'm going to leave four agents outside in vehicles, and Abigail..." Perry motioned to an agent pulling a bag out of the back of one of the SUVs. "She will be staying in the house overnight."

"Sounds good." Josh stood and turned to the door. "I'll let Nikki know what's going on." He just hoped she'd be open to it.

A minute later, he found her in the kitchen and relayed the news.

She frowned.

"I know it'll be a bit weird, but Perry just wants to make sure you're safe."

She rolled her eyes. "Fine."

Wanting to lighten the mood, Josh shot her a grin. "Still want to get married and disappear?"

Nikki turned back to washing the teacups and saucers in the old farmhouse sink. "My brother is out there somewhere. After finally learning he exists, I don't want to abandon him. I want to know that he's safe. I want to find him again."

"But we don't have any idea where he is."

Moving up behind her, Josh slid his palms over her shoulders and gently squeezed. His intention was to help her relax, but she seemed to stiffen under his touch and pulled away to get a dish towel from a drawer.

"Is something wrong?"

"Have you not been here for the last hour?" She let out a wry laugh. "A lot of things are wrong."

"What I meant was, is something wrong between you and me?"

"Of course not."

The answer came quickly. *Too quickly.* Josh watched as she kept her stare fixed on the foamy suds. She was lying or at least trying to make something true that her mind told her wasn't. The instinct to interrogate rose within him. *I can get it out of her.*

After all, he was a sheriff's deputy and a former MP during part of his military career. A good one. His mind was already forming the questions he was going to throw at her until he remembered the time when he'd actually seen her interrogated by the police not all that long ago.

45

The sheriff hadn't held back with his accusations and intimidation tactics as she sat frightened and shaking in the cold, metal seat in the sheriff's department interrogation room. Josh had had to watch the whole thing transpire from the other side of the two-way glass. Never would he forget the torment on her face during the ordeal.

How could he be the cause of such torture now? She was hiding something. That was clear. But he wasn't going to try to trick or force it out of her. She would tell him when she was ready... he hoped.

He took the dish towel she'd tossed over her shoulder. "I thought I'd stay as well and help with the dishes. Then... I could sleep on the couch so I can be here if anything happens."

Nikki turned on the faucet and rinsed a saucer, still turned away from him. "I really don't think that's necessary. Abigail is here." She tilted her head towards the den where the female marshal sat. "Between her and the agents outside, I'm sure I will be fine."

"Nikki, can you at least look at me?"

She put the dish in the drying rack and faced him. Her deep blue eyes were finally on him, but there was a hint of unrecognition in her expression. It hurt. And worse, he saw no reason for the sudden change. He wanted to be angry, but... "You know I love you, right?"

The uncertainty lingered for a moment longer but then seemed to fade a bit, replaced by the genuine affection he was used to seeing.

"I know." She took one step, her surrender compelling him to banish any space between them.

He pulled her close, running his fingers along her jaw before firmly grasping the back of her neck. He let his forehead drop to rest on hers and then closed his eyes as he listened to the cadence of their breathing.

She sighed. "I know."

CHAPTER 6

HE MUST BE WRONG.

Nikki watched from her front door as Josh's patrol car pulled away. Her brother must be wrong. Of course, she could trust Josh. He was the most honest man she knew, but still those foreboding words etched on that paper were now etched on her mind. Rob couldn't possibly have meant her fiancé. *Josh* hadn't cut the brake lines on her truck, set her shop on fire, and hold her at gunpoint. Rob must just think—incorrectly—that Josh was another bad apple because of his association with the sheriff's department. Or he was confusing him for the real bad guy.

What am I supposed to think? Her brother had said he came here to make sure she was safe, so he must care about her. But if he was telling her that the man she planned to marry didn't have her best intentions in mind, she couldn't agree. Before tonight, she hadn't even known she had a brother, but she'd known Josh since she'd moved to St. Claire. Would she really take a stranger's word over his? She squeezed her eyes shut, trying to picture Rob's face. Was her father's image in there somewhere? She couldn't be sure. If they'd only had more time before he ran off.

"You okay, Miss Appleton?" Abigail asked.

Nikki realized she'd been standing in her entry way, staring awkwardly at her still-open door. "Yeah." She recovered her composure and closed it. "Just a lot to think about."

48

"Of course, it is." The other woman reached back and pulled her dark ponytail tight. "I've cleared the upstairs if you'd like to turn in. If you hear steps down here, don't get alarmed. I'll be walking the house regularly until my relief comes in the morning."

It was surprising to Nikki how young the marshal was. If not for the dark blazer and dress pants she was wearing, the woman would look like she should be getting back to her dorm before lights out. "I'm so sorry you have to stay up for what's left of the night. You have to be exhausted."

"All part of the job." Abigail winked a bright blue eye. "You can rest easy."

Abigail's relaxed manner was a breath of fresh air. Either the agent wasn't worried about any danger or she was confident she could handle it. Nikki was fine with either possibility. She was beat, physically and emotionally. "Sounds like a plan." She stifled a yawn and turned to the stairs. Two steps up, she turned back. "Hey, Abigail?"

"Yes, Miss Appleton?"

"Nikki, please. Miss Appleton makes me sound ancient, and we're probably about the same age."

"Of course, Nikki." She chuckled. "What can I do for you?"

"I was wondering. Do you know my brother?"

She shook her head. "No. I was never on his detail."

"I see. I guess I was trying to get some kind of clue as to what he's like."

A dimple appeared in the marshal's bottom lip as she chewed it from the inside. "I really couldn't tell you. But I'm sure you'll be meeting the lead assigned to his case soon. Since Robert's missing, he will certainly want to talk to you."

Missing. She shivered. A lot of the time, missing people became dead people.

Abigail rested a hand on the banister. "I wouldn't be too worried about him, though. I have familiarized myself with his file, and the one thing I know about Robert Appleton is that he's smart. The family he was placed with had to move his freshman year of high school because Rob hacked into one of his teacher's computers to prove the teacher was helping students cheat on their standardized tests."

Nikki recalled the note taped to the back of the photograph in her pocket. The quick thinking it would've taken to write. The warning spelled out for her. If Rob was that smart, should she really ignore what he had said about Josh? "Wow."

"I know." Abigail nodded. "The local news got wind of it, so they had to get him out fast. As you can probably guess, media attention is the bane of WITSEC."

"I-I can see why it would be." She bit her lip. With all the cameras that had been pointed at her during the grand reopening, Josh might as well have held up a sign saying *She's in St. Claire.* His proposal—romantic as it was— practically made the day go viral. It wasn't just the newspaper after that. The local news interviewed her. People shared the video on the internet. What if he'd done it on purpose? Could Josh have been sending a message to her brother?

"If Robert went on the run…" Abigail crossed her other arm over the banister, too, and laid her chin on her wrist. "He must have had a good reason."

"Thanks for trying to make me feel better." Nikki plastered on a smile. "I should probably get to sleep."

"Goodnight, Miss… Nikki."

Nikki chuckled. "Goodnight, Abigail."

The kittens did not hold back when she turned the glass doorknob to her room. Their barrage of meows and mewling seemed to be half raptures of joy at seeing her and half furious rebukes at being closed up in there for so long and then not let free when she'd come up to change. She hurriedly swapped out her jeans for pajama shorts and then scooped up Meg, scratching the strips of black fur between her ears.

Her motherless gray fur babies—discovered in her shop after the break-in—were growing bigger every day.

Not bothering to hold back a yawn, Nikki pulled back the corner of her quilt and crawled into bed. Jo and Amy followed her up, climbing up the side of the blanket with their little claws. Nikki sank into the mattress, feeling their vibrating little bodies curling up against her. Jo hopped up to the head of the bed and bopped Nikki's face with her whiskery nose.

Nikki chuckled. "You know you guys are going to have to make some room in here if Josh moves in, you know?" Why had she said *if* and not *when*? Tears blurred her view. The thought of not sharing a home with Josh drew a sob from her lips. She thought back to the embrace in the kitchen. She pictured the moment his forehead was against hers. And the heat between them as they breathed like they were melded together. Smart or not, Rob had to be wrong about him.

After wiping away the tears, she looked into Jo's curious eyes. "You think Josh loves me, right?" Jo's response was to plop down next to her face on the pillow. Nikki gave her a scratch behind the ear and then leaned over and switched on the desk fan on her night stand and closed her eyes. Sleeping in empty silence had always been hard for her, but with the gentle hum of the fan and the rumbling purring of the kittens, sleep came quickly.

Sometime later, Nikki awakened to the uneasy feeling that something had changed. Was it too hot? Or too quiet? Forcing her eyes open, she shifted under the bedding and reached for the switch on her fan.

Her fingers found the switch on the base of the fan and flicked. Nothing. After trying it again with the same result, she reached for the lamp but found that it was dead too. A tight knot formed in her chest. Something was wrong. Tired no more, she sat up straight and held her breath as she listened to a soft creak reminiscent of footfalls on the old wooden floors going down the stairs to the main floor.

An internal voice told her not to panic. After all, Abigail had told her not to worry if she heard walking. But why was the power out? Relieving herself of the quilt, Nikki got to her feet and crept to her open bedroom door. Peering around the frame, she looked for a glimpse of light downstairs, but all she saw was black. Her body told her to sound the alarm, and she briefly considered throwing open her bedroom window and screaming to the other marshals parked outside, but what if the power was only out because of the earlier thunderstorm?

Summoning her courage, Nikki called down the hall. "Abigail?"

The only response was a sudden burst of light behind her. She yelped. Once again, her fan was buzzing and her lamp, now shone into the darkness.

Blinking, she tried to acclimate herself to the light as she moved to the stairs. "Abigail?" It must have been the weather that had temporarily knocked out the electricity. But why wasn't Abigail answering?

Maybe she had fallen asleep. Obviously, the marshal was supposed to stay awake, but Nikki wouldn't blame her if she'd nodded off. Except, then, whose footsteps had she heard creaking downstairs?

On her tiptoes, she crept down the stairs, but before she could call out again, she heard a thud and a woman's cry from the direction of the basement stairs. Abigail. Nikki remembered how narrow that staircase was. It would be easy to slip and fall. Everything went black as the power once again disappeared.

Nikki bolted in the direction of the noise. Navigating through the house more from memory than sight, she staggered through the basement door and down the narrow staircase, bracing herself with her hands on the walls.

"Abigail! Are you okay?" If only she could see. She could go back to the kitchen for her flashlight, except the breaker box was only a few feet ahead on the wall nearby. She stuck out her palms and stumbled in that direction. "Oof!" Her foot had caught on something and sent her sprawling.

A shock of pain rattled her arm as her elbow bashed onto the concrete. She gasped as she landed on something that knocked the wind out of her. What was that? What had tripped her? Her flailing hands found something lumpy. It was as big as a person. Wait... It was a person! Nikki scrambled to the side, scared she'd hurt whoever was on the ground. A low moan came from the lump.

Taking an educated guess as to the person's identity, Nikki called out. "Abigail! Abigail, can you hear me?" The agent groaned and her body shifted. *Thank you, Jesus.*

"Don't move yet, okay. You're injured and I don't know how bad it is." Nikki reached for her face. The agent's cheeks were warm, and her eyes were fluttering. Nikki ran her fingers up the line of her nose up to her forehead. They got caught in something warm and sticky. Blood.

Oh God, please let her be okay. How could she hope to help the agent in this pitch blackness? And what had happened? Nikki got to her feet and began feeling for the breaker box. Cringing when her fingers passed through spider webs, she persevered. But just when she felt the cool metal edge of the box, a rustling noise came from behind.

Nikki froze. She and Abigail were not alone. Abandoning the electrical box, she searched around her for some kind of weapon in the clutter of the who-knew-what she'd haphazardly stored there. There had to be something she could use to defend herself. But would she find it in time?

Just as her right hand wrapped around the heavy handle of some mystery object, a hand grabbed her left arm and jerked her backwards. Nikki lost her footing and went spiraling over the agent, but she was determined not to go easy. Kicking, fighting, and blindly swinging her weapon, she battled, desperate for her freedom as the attacker dragged her away from the stairs.

Over the sound of her screamed protests, she heard him grunting in frustration as their struggle inched slowly towards the back of the basement. Suddenly, she knew where they were headed. He was trying to take her out the storm doors that led to the outside. Nikki's memories jumped to the last time someone had dragged her away from the back of her house. "No!"

Her hip hit the bottom step of the short climb to the outside. A hand clamped around her thrashing hand and shook it, sending her mystery weapon clattering to the floor. He jerked her into him and stabbed his hands under her arms when she heard a rush of steps overhead. Nikki's heart leapt with joy.

"I'M DOWN HERE!" Hopefully it was the marshals upstairs and not more dark figures come to help steal her away into the night.

The stranger's hold on her was stronger than ever as his feet climbed the stairs with loud thuds. A rush of cool air hit her as the storm doors swung open and her attacker pulled her into the darkness. Stray rocks and sticks in the grass poked at her bare feet as he dragged her into the tree line. Brush scratched at her arms as she was pulled through the woods.

Her attacker was breathing heavily and grunting as they moved. He was slowing down. Maybe she still had a chance to escape. She reached over her head smacking and scratching at his face. If she could stall him, even for a moment, it would give the Marshals time to get to her.

Kicking out with her feet, she tried wrapping her legs around branches and tree limbs until her right leg hooked around the thin trunk of a tree and she held on with all her strength.

The sudden jolt must have surprised her attacker because he let out an exclamation and fell forward. Nikki felt his arms slide out from under her and she was sent sprawling to the ground.

Nikki struggled to stand, her feet fighting against the mud trying to swallow her into the forest floor. She started to run but got caught on the raised loop of a tree root and went down once again.

Jumping upright, she realized she'd lost her bearings, her sense of direction, and—most importantly—sight of her attacker. Had she proved too much of a burden? Had he given up on his kidnapping attempt and fled?

It was too dark and he could be anywhere. She needed to calm down and find the way back home. Trying to steady her breathing, she listened for any noise that would get her back on the right track. She only heard the wind picking up and a rumble of thunder in the distance. Another storm was coming? And she was bleeding, bruised, burnt, and utterly alone.

A branch snapped behind her.

Oh no. He was still there.

Lord, help me.

CHAPTER 7

NIKKI'S BLOODCURDLING SCREAM WHEN JOSH grabbed her sent him into a panic. "It's me." Instead of calming down, she fought to get away from him. "It's Josh, honey."

Why wouldn't she stop fighting? He prayed he didn't hurt her. "I'm here."

He managed to get his arms around her in an encasing bear hug. "It's all right. You're safe." She seemed to still, then twisted to look into his face. It was dark, but since he could make out her features, he prayed she could see his, too, and know she was safe.

Her brow furrowed, and a look of relief graced her features causing him to loosen his hold. But as quickly as the peace had come, it vanished, terror taking its place.

She pushed him back, forcing him away with her palms on his chest. "You left. I-I saw you leave. You went home, but now you're here? Why are you here?"

She was rambling and stumbling backwards to get away from him. Would anything he said even get through to her? He followed her.

"Josh, why are you out here?" She pushed on his chest, grunting at him.

Josh held out his hands. Take it slow. "I went home to change into something clean and dry." He motioned to his black shirt and jeans. "Then, I came back. I was outside with the marshals when we saw the lights in your bedroom flash on and off during a strong wind. When Abigail didn't report that the house was secure, we went in. You called out from the basement, but when I got down there, you were gone."

Her eyes went blank as her mind worked. Did she actually doubt his story? Where had this sudden suspicion come from? Just now she'd looked at him like she didn't know him. Like he was there to hurt her. What had he done to cause this heartbreaking shift?

"I got free. He was trying to pull me away." She motioned to the woods behind her.

Him? "Who?" His heart skipped a beat. Why had he left? Had Rob come back for her or had it been someone worse?

"The man that was in my house. When the power went out, I went downstairs to make sure Abigail was okay, but I found her in the..." She clutched at his arms. "Oh, my goodness! Is she okay? I think she was bleeding when I found her."

"I think so. She was sitting up when I got down there." Josh said through gritted teeth. How could a trained marshal and a perimeter of her teammates have let someone slip in unnoticed? Josh blinked, catching sight of dozens of flashlights through the trees. "When I saw the open storm doors, I took off. But it looks like I wasn't the only one to chase you down. That will be the marshals."

She dug her fingers into his skin. "We have to make sure she's okay. He must have attacked her when she went down into the basement to check the power. She must have turned it back on but then been hurt. He was in the basement when I got down there."

Josh pulled her to his chest, wrapping her in his arms.

58

"Is WITSEC sounding a little better right about now?" Perry's angry voice cut in. "We could all be in bed right now instead of trekking through the mud."

"Go easy on her." Josh turned putting his back between Nikki and the marshal. Then he leaned his head back to look down into her eyes. "Do you know which direction he went?"

She stepped backwards and spun in a circle. "Um… not really. I-I fell and lost sight of him. I could barely see him to begin with. Just a dark outline of a person. Maybe that way." She pointed deeper into the woods.

"Fan out!" Perry yelled to his men and then turned to Nikki. "Let's get you secure." Rubbing her arms like she was trying to stop a chill, she nodded. "Is Abigail okay?" Nikki's teeth chattered.

"I think she will be." Perry's hand fell to the radio clipped to his belt. "I had an agent stay behind and call an ambulance, but you were the priority. Now that I know you're safe, we'll concentrate all our efforts on the pursuit."

Stepping up to Josh, Nikki twisted the fabric of his shirt in her fists. "Don't go after him. Stay with me. We have to make sure she's okay."

Josh raised a hand to her cheek. Her skin was ice cold against his palm. "I'm not going anywhere. I'm right here with you." Draping an arm across her shoulder, he turned her towards the house and pulled her into his side. He led her towards the house.

As they moved, Josh glanced at the ground and saw her bare feet sinking into the wet and freezing grass as she jogged to keep pace.

Would she let him carry her? He recalled the last time he'd carried her. At Apple's with the shop burning down around them. He'd been trying to save her, but she hadn't trusted him then either. Especially when he handed her to her ex-boyfriend, a man they'd suspected of trying to kill her.

Josh had understood her doubts then. But now he wondered if it had been more than that. Had she thought he was handing her over to her killer because he was in league with the convict somehow? Josh shuddered. Could she really think such a thing about him?

Nikki broke free from him when they reached the first step. He caught the screen door as she threw it open and pushed her way inside without him.

Was the wall she'd had around her heart when they'd first met still there? *She loves me, Lord. I know she does. But what if she doesn't trust me? What if she'll never trust me?*

***

"Thank God you're okay." Nikki fell onto one of the chairs around her kitchen table. Abigail sat in the chair next to her being examined by Tuck, a local EMT who stopped at her shop a lot when he was on shift.

The agent moved a light-colored towel that was quickly turning pink from her brow and met Nikki's eyes. "I can't believe that guy got the drop on me. I'm so sorry I didn't stop him."

Nikki motioned to her face. Like her own, Abigail's skin was milky white, but even if it had been tanned from summer, the bright, red blood streaked down the one side of her face from a gash on her forehead would still be stark and shocking. "It wasn't your fault. You were pretty out of it. Look what he did to you."

Nikki heard squeaking and turned to see Josh closing the back door. He frowned in Abigail's direction. "Ouch."

Abigail snorted and returned the towel to her wound. "Tell me about it."

Josh stepped past Nikki's chair, dragging his fingers along the tabletop as he stepped up to Tuck. "You guys got here fast, man."

Nikki squinted at the uniformed man as he chuckled. "You've given me enough speeding tickets to know I got a lead foot, deputy."

Nikki smiled. "Thank you for coming so soon. I know I'm kind of out here and she needed help fast."

Tuck pulled a penlight from the front pocket of his shirt. "Well, it's about time you saw me doing something other than stuffing my face with doughnuts." He shone the light down into Abigail's eye line. "Now, let's see the damage. Go ahead and look at me, ma'am."

Abigail lifted her chin to the light. It flashed in and out of both of her eyes as Tuck stared, biting his bottom lip. "Do you know your name?"

"Abigail," she said with a sigh.

Tuck opened his mouth to ask another question, but she cut him off.

"I work for the US Marshals. I'm currently in Nadine County, Pennsylvania working under the command of Perry Cole. That enough?"

Tuck pursed his lips. "Well, your pupil reactions look okay, but I think you should come with me and my partner to the hospital. The doctors will want to rule out anything serious. We don't take head injuries lightly."

The marshal groaned. "Is that really necessary? I'm sure I can tough it out."

St. Claire police officer Mike Whittaker sauntered into the kitchen. "I never met a woman who couldn't. But I'm guessing if your boss comes back and you're still here, he'll just drive you to the hospital himself."

Abigail rolled her eyes. "Fine." She stood to her feet but then wobbled like she'd moved too fast.

Tuck grabbed her arm, steadying her. "Easy. Let's take it slow."

Not too long ago, Nikki had been the one wobbling on her feet after an accident. She winced in sympathy, recalling how the world could spin.

With Tuck's assistance, Abigail turned and started towards the door, nodding to Mike as she left.

Nikki followed them out onto the porch and waved a hand to Abigail as Tuck helped her climb up into the back of the ambulance parked on the grass just below the porch steps.

Tuck pulled one of the doors closed, then paused. "You might see me in a bit. I'm gonna stop by for some jelly doughnuts before I head home."

Nikki watched the other door shut and the ambulance pull down her bumpy driveway to the country road. Josh stepped past her and put his hands on the porch rail. "A French cruller dunked in coffee does sound good about now."

His favorite.

Oh no. Nikki flinched. *"Crullers.* Oh gosh. What time is it? I have to open the shop." She turned to the front door and found Perry stepping over the threshold. She brushed past him, charging towards the kitchen, her eyes looking out for the swinging tail of her cat clock as she made her way down the hall.

2:45 a.m.

She needed to be at Apple's by three thirty. She glanced down at her body. The parts of her legs and feet that weren't blackened with dirt and mud were still red and burning from the boiling tea water that had spilled on her. Her pajamas were damp. And she needed a shower. Like now. Nikki spun around to sprint to the stairs.

"Oof!" She hit something. Taking a step back so as not to fall, she looked up to find Josh. He raised an eyebrow.

What was his problem?

"What do you think you are doing?" He crossed his arms over his chest.

Over Josh's shoulder she saw Perry closing her front door and turning the deadbolt lock. "Er… I'm going to shower. I have to leave for work soon."

Josh untwisted his arms and pushed the sleeves of his black henley styled shirt up to his elbows. "You're going to work?"

There was no time to argue about this. Nikki pushed her ratty, wet hair behind her ears. "Why wouldn't I?"

His other eyebrow joined the first, and he tilted his head like he was trying to determine if, while trying to escape the basement, she had conked her head. "Because it's not safe?"

Nikki glanced at Mike in the kitchen and Perry behind Josh. Both of the other men looked tense. "And it's so safe here?"

Josh drove a hand into his blond hair that looked closer to brown when it was damp like now. "Someone just tried to kidnap you. He could still be out there."

Nikki stepped to her left so she stood before Perry. There was no talking to Josh when his protective nature took over. She'd have better luck with the marshal. "You have people all through the woods, Perry. Did anyone catch the guy?"

Perry's eyes flicked to Josh and then fell to the floor. "No."

Just as she thought. Nikki shrugged. "Then, I'm thinking he's gone."

Perry cleared his throat. "That doesn't mean you should go out into the night and potentially run into him. With Rob missing and the Snitch possibly out there—"

"We don't even know if the intruder had anything to do with any of that." Her hands went to her hips. "You didn't come to Apple's to warn me about the Snitch. You came to warn me about a Pittsburgh police officer who had a bunch of pictures of me. It could've just been him coming after me out of revenge or something. And now that he knows there's an army of marshals around me, he'd have to be stupid to try anything again."

Josh stepped close to her, cupping her cheek with one hand and pulling her close with the other. She saw Perry out of the corner of her eye and blood rushed to her face at the thought of having an audience. However, she loved that

Josh didn't shy away from making his feelings known. There were no games with Josh Bennet.

"You don't know that he won't come back. It's not safe."

She nuzzled against his palm and sighed. "You'll protect me."

His breath caught. "I can't. I have to work, too. I can't be with you all the time."

Nikki's stomach churned, and she closed her eyes. She hadn't thought of that. Josh had responsibilities to the town and couldn't just take off work. But could she really not show up? She could not expect Beverly, the retired teacher who worked for her, to be ready at the drop of the hat. Besides, even if she was available on such short notice, there was too much prep work to be done. Work Nikki normally did ahead of time on the few occasions the older woman opened for her. The older woman couldn't handle that on her own.

She opened her eyes and swallowed hard. "I-I still have to go. I just reopened. I didn't do any prep yesterday. I can't afford to lose a day's business and Beverly's not prepared to open without me."

His body tensed, and his previously warm eyes darkened. How far would he would go to stop her?

Perry groaned next them. "You go to work, deputy. Me and your local guy will keep an eye out for your girlfriend."

Nikki flashed the marshal a smile. "Fiancée."

CHAPTER 8

AFTER SPENDING THE MORNING PATROLLING the back-country roads, Josh slowed and steered into a popular pull-off spot. His tires bumped over the gravel-mud mixture, and the bare tree branches shook water onto his windshield. The rain had stopped, and the unseasonably warm weather had been replaced with bitter cold. Parts of the roads were sheets of ice. It would be easy for a driver to underestimate their speed, hit black ice, and go spinning. Most of the winding roads and hills had guard rails, but to lose control on one that didn't meant a deadly trip down a steep drop. *Lord, protect the drivers.*

Once parked, Josh grabbed his phone off the empty passenger seat so he could text Perry for about the fiftieth time since he'd started his shift.

ALL OKAY AT APPLE'S?

Josh tapped on the steering wheel as he waited for a reply. His muscles tightened with every minute that passed without response. Should he drive over there himself? Deciding to call the bakery line, he had just opened his contacts when a response finally came.

SAME AS WHEN YOU ASKED TEN MINUTES AGO. MIKE IS ON HIS FIFTH DOUBLE CHOCOLATE DOUGHNUT.

Josh grunted. No way would they make him feel bad for worrying about his future wife. The marshal would just have to deal. Josh had just started tapping out a curt reply

66

when a blue blur whooshed past him. With one hand, he flipped on his flashing lights while tossing his phone—message unsent—back on the seat with the other. His back tires spun as he sped out onto the road in pursuit.

Through the back window of the blue sedan, Josh saw the moment the driver realized he'd been caught. His head swiveled to his mirror and then fell back against the seat. No one liked finding out they were about to get a ticket. *Well, you should have thought about that before speeding.*

But would the driver pull over or try to make a run for it? He had only been in a few car chases, but those few were enough. People got hurt in chases, usually bystanders.

As the vehicle pulled off the side of the road, Josh let out a relieved sigh and parked his patrol car just behind. He squinted at the license plate, then pulled his radio off the dash to relay the numbers to dispatch. It wasn't stolen, which was always a concern but it did come back as a rental out of Pittsburgh. The hairs on the back of his neck stood on end. Who rented a car in Pittsburgh and then drove down to Nadine county? Was this the missing police officer who had stalked Nikki? It was no stretch of the imagination to wonder if a new face in town meant bad news. After all, there wasn't all that that much to see, especially in the winter when the very tiny amusement park outside town closed down leaving only the Amish shops and bakeries to attract tourists.

After he thanked dispatch for the information, Josh elbowed his door open, tossing the receiver onto the passenger seat. Glancing back to check for oncoming traffic, Josh started towards the speeder. Rocks and uneven road crunched under his feet. The side mirror was flashing red and blue as it reflected the lights of the patrol car and the driver's side window was sliding open as Josh approached.

"Afternoon, officer."

Josh palmed his holster. "Afternoon." The driver was young. Maybe twenty-five. But the white dress shirt and tie made it clear he was well out of college. "I clocked you at sixty-two."

"Is that not the speed limit?" The man smirked.

"Forty-five." Josh pulled his ticket book from his belt. "I'll need your license and registration."

The man grabbed his suit jacket, which was thrown carelessly over the head rest of the passenger side seat.

"Easy now." Josh unsnapped his holster and wrapped his hand around the grip of his gun.

The man froze with his hand in the air, the blazer sticking out of his closed fist. "I'm just getting my wallet. It's in the inside pocket."

"How about you let me get it then?" Josh held out his left hand. When the man draped it across his palm, Josh drew it to his chest and stuck a hand into the breast pocket. He pulled out a black, leather billfold.

He flipped it open and ran his finger over the gold-plated badge inside. "This isn't a license..." Just what St. Claire needed. "You need to slow down, Special Agent Sterling."

First the Marshals and now the FBI? Who was next? The National Guard?

The agent shrugged. "I got that too." He held up a smooth plastic card between two fingers.

What's he doing all the way down here? Was this the FBI Agent that helped Perry look into the stalker? Josh raised an eyebrow and snatched the man's license. "You thinking because you're FBI, I'm not going to give you a ticket?"

The agent held up his hands like a gun was pointed at him. "Never. Here, I'll get you the registration." He pushed the button on the glove box, and when it fell open, grabbed the packet of papers inside and handed it over. "I'm assuming the rental company has everything in order. And I just wanted you to know we're cut from the same cloth. If that happens to lead to you letting me off the hook... so be it."

Josh tore the ticket sheet off the book and handed it to the agent. "What's the FBI doing all the way out here?"

The agent grimaced as he read the ticket, probably wincing at the steep fine. "Meeting a marshal friend of mine. Think he'll pay my ticket? I am doing him a favor, after all."

That couldn't be a coincidence. "Is your friend Perry Cole?"

The agent started. "You know Perry?"

This guy could be lying for some reason. Maybe it would be better to play things close to the vest. "We've worked together a bit."

Agent Sterling's brow furrowed. "Wait. You're not the baker's boyfriend, are you?"

Josh let out a slow breath. Perry had said it was an FBI friend who had discovered the missing police officer and his wall of photographs, but how did Josh know this was him? Should he answer? Was this guy trustworthy or fishing for a way to get close to Nikki?

"I get it, man." He waved Josh off. "You don't know me and aren't going to start giving me information. Perry can vouch for me if I can find him. He didn't answer my last call. Any chance you know where he is right now?"

Josh cleared his throat and then handed the man back his badge, license, and registration. "Follow me. I imagine you should have no trouble keeping up."

***

"If you eat any more of these, you're going to get a stomachache." Nikki reached across the counter to hand Mike another small, hand-painted plate topped with a double chocolate doughnut.

He grinned as he took it in his hand. "Worth it."

Tilting her head, she looked past Mike's shoulder to where Perry sipped the last of his coffee at a corner table. "Perry, do you want another éclair?"

He shook his head and patted his stomach. "No more doughnuts for me, but I'll take some more coffee if you don't mind."

"Sure thing." Nikki turned and grabbed the black handle of the glass pot from under the drip. Careful not to spill, she followed Mike over to the marshal's table.

Mike sat down across from him as Nikki began to pour and breathed in the fragrance of the dark roast as it splashed into Perry's cup. She could use another cup herself. After all, it had been a long night and a long morning, and she was both dragging and guilt-filled that Perry and Mike were stuck keeping an eye on her.

She wished it was Josh sitting here. Wished she could feel his hand cup her neck or her cheek or feel the tingling sensation that coursed across her skin whenever he whispered something alluring into her ear. But he wasn't here.

"Thanks for being here, Perry. I know you put Josh's mind at ease."

"You'd think." Perry nudged his cell phone on the table with a finger. "But the fifty texts I've got from him over the last few hours say otherwise."

Nikki wiped her free hand over her face. "Oh jeez. I'm sorry. He's probably driving you crazy. It's just that he, uh…"

"Loves you?" Mike mumbled, his mouth full of doughnut.

Her brother's message flashed in her mind. *Don't trust the deputy. Did* Josh love her? Or was he just keeping tabs on her for some unknown nefarious reason? And if his love was a lie, was her faith a lie too? After all, it'd been Josh who had led her to God.

"Of course." But how sure about that was she? Tucking a strand of hair behind her ear, she turned to see if any other customers needed a refill. Things that seemed so certain just hours ago, now seemed up in the air.

She remembered the moment she'd surrendered everything she had to the Lord. Trapped in the trunk of a car and being taken away from everything she loved, Nikki hadn't known if she was going to live or die, but then suddenly, she knew she wasn't alone. She knew that live or die, God was in control. She couldn't imagine a peace like that, could she? It had surpassed her understanding. It transformed her thinking. The calm in the midst of that awful storm couldn't have been a lie. Josh may have pointed her in the right direction but faith had been her choice alone.

Nikki made her way to the table where Anna Duncan, the owner of the nearby Poppy's Pies, Tarts, and Cobblers, sat alone, an open book in her hand.

"Well, I'm jealous."

Anna jumped in surprise and then put her hand on her chest as she chuckled. "You scared me. What did you say?"

She should've given her a bit of warning. The poor girl's face had gone as pale as the eggshell scarf knotted around her neck. "I'm so sorry. I didn't mean to sneak up on you. I just said that I'm jealous of you."

Anna pursed her lips. "Why?"

Maybe she shouldn't have blurted that out. What if Anna took offense? Maybe she should just say she was jealous of the woman's fair hair with its natural highlights. No. Probably best to just go with the whole truth. "Oh, it's nothing. You're just here drinking coffee and reading a book during business hours. I feel like I *never* get out of here.

Anna's mouth split into a sympathetic smile. "That's because it's just you running your shop. Poppy's was handed down to me. I've got cousins, aunts, and siblings I can put to work. You're doing an awesome job though. Everyone loves it here."

There was yet another reason having a family was important. They were people to be counted on. Would she have had to work her fingers to the bone if she had a family that loved her and was there to help? She did have help though. Lizzy and Josh had been there for most of the construction. But could she really call them her family with things being the way they were? She didn't want to think about that right now.

"Thanks. Can I top you off?" She motioned to the pot in her hand.

Anna's eyes brightened. "Yes, please."

Nikki let the remainder of the steaming coffee fall into the cup on the table. "Sorry again for interrupted. You must have been pretty engrossed in your book. Must be a pretty good story."

Anna lifted the cup with her palms and blew, causing the mocha colored pool to ripple. "It is. I'm a sucker for suspense."

Nikki pulled a tea towel from the pocket of her checkered apron and wiped away a stray drop running down the glass of the coffee pot. "Not me. Life is suspenseful enough. I'll take a sweet romance over thrill and danger any day." The way Josh stared into her eyes right before kissing her popped into her mind. Shaking the thought away, she forced her lips into a smile. "Well, I better go make some more of this coffee. I'll talk to you later."

"Bye, Nikki."

When she rounded the corner of the counter, Nikki nodded to Beverly. "I'm going to put on another pot."

The older woman handed some bills to a customer and then pushed the cash drawer closed. "There's no more regular coffee beans out here. Just decaf. I was just about to run back to the kitchen and get some."

"I'll do it." Nikki set the empty pot on one of the warming plates that had cooled and pushed through the swinging doors to the kitchen. A blast of icy air hit her skin. Why was the back door open? Goose pimples crawled up her arms and it wasn't just because of the cold. Mike and

Perry were just a few feet away. Should she call out? Or turn around and get them?

She sucked in a breath. Why the overreaction because of a simple door? Beverly often forgot to check the latch when she used it.

Get a grip. Since it was open, Nikki decided she might as well take out some of the trash. Jogging across the kitchen, she grabbed the nearly full bag from the bin on the far side of the island, and twisted the top into a knot before throwing it over her shoulder.

Just as she passed the long silver bar across the heavy green door, Nikki caught a glimpse of a shadow on the pavement and yelped. Was there someone behind the door? Maybe the man from last night?

Loose gravel kicked up as whoever it was took a step back as if they'd been startled. Why would the man from last night be scared of her? Why didn't he charge at her to make another attempt?

Could it be... *Rob*? What if he was trying to get her another message? Another picture that would give her another clue to her past? He could've seen Perry through the windows out front and decided to wait for her out here. If that was him, she had to talk to him again, but if she called out to Perry, she was certain he'd run. There were so many questions he could answer. She had to try and get the chance to ask them. Nikki dropped the trash bag and stepped around the door.

Her foot came down in a half frozen puddle, and cold water splashed her shins as she rounded the open door. She saw no one but heard footsteps retreating around the side of the building.

"*Wait.*"

The footsteps stopped.

"Rob?" Her heart beat faster.

The steps started again, but this time, they were growing louder. Whoever was out there was coming towards her. Just like in her basement only hours before when rough hands had dragged her across the floor. The memory of being dragged away from her home flashed in her mind.

Was this a mistake? Had her step of faith landed her into the man from last night's trap? It wasn't too late. She just had to get back inside. Broken asphalt scraped the sole of her tennis shoes as she spun back around, but before she could take another step, a car came from the other side of the building.

She let out a breath. It was a Nadine County sheriff's car and her fiancé was behind the wheel. Nikki glanced back over her shoulder for the shadow she feared was coming. It wasn't just her the bad guy would be facing anymore. A car door shut, and she turned. Flutters danced across her chest as she watched Josh and all his bulk strolling her way. How could she have doubts about such an enticing man?

CHAPTER 9

"WHAT ARE YOU DOING STANDING out here in the cold?" Josh sloughed off his department issued winter coat and wrapped it around Nikki's small frame.

She pushed her arm through the sleeves. "I-I went to the kitchen to get coffee beans, and the back door was open. I thought I heard someone and came out to look."

Alone? Did she not realize she was in danger? "You shouldn't have come out here by yourself. It could have been the guy from last night."

She chewed her bottom lip, and her chin dropped to her chest like she was embarrassed that she hadn't thought of that. "I was just taking the trash out when I heard something. I thought it could have been my brother trying to talk to me alone." She looked over his shoulder. "Who is that?"

Josh glanced back. Agent Sterling had parked his rental next to Josh's cruiser in the small lot and now walked towards them. "The FBI friend Perry talked about. The one who found those pictures on the missing cop's wall."

Nikki scrunched up her face. "What's he doing *here*?"

"Good question." Josh looked up and saw Perry had just joined them outside. "I don't remember calling you, Luke."

Agent Sterling brushed past Josh, moving towards the marshal. "Like you're not glad to see me."

Perry rolled his eyes. "The FBI must really be desperate for work if they're sending you down here. But I guess since you're here, you can help me keep an eye on this one." He nodded at Nikki.

Agent Sterling looked back at Nikki and grinned. "She doesn't look all that dangerous to me."

Perry blew a hard breath through his lips and crossed his arms. "She's a flight risk. Went for coffee and never came back. Got a penchant for running off."

Josh's chest tightened. She *did* tend to disappear. And sometimes it was by choice. He remembered the night he had discovered her sneaking off on her own because she thought it would be safer for *him*. She'd let him change her mind, but what if he hadn't found her? That night could've ended with her in the hospital instead of with their first kiss. His pulsed quickened as he relived that blissful moment when he couldn't hold back his feelings for another second and had pulled her to him, letting his lips crash into hers.

He shook the enticing memory away. Now wasn't the time.

Red faced, Nikki groaned. "I was only gone for a minute."

Perry raised an eyebrow. "Yeah and nothing bad can happen in a minute."

Nikki scoffed and then opened her mouth to reply but Josh laid his hand on her shoulder. "He's right. You shouldn't have come out here alone."

She pursed her lips. "We don't know why my brother ran last night, but if I had gotten the marshals, he might have run again or just disappeared while I was walking back to the dining room. I didn't want to miss a chance to find him." She waved a hand towards the start of the mulch covered path running along the right side of the building.

When she shrugged off his hand, Josh dropped his arm to his side and stuck a thumb in his utility belt. "And what if it wasn't your brother?"

Her tongue clicked as she shot him a glare. "But what if it was? I'm not fighting about this. My brother is out there, and I'm going to do whatever I can to find him."

Josh stepped up into her personal space. "You can't find him if you're taken or killed."

"Let's take a time out." Perry cut in, grabbing Josh's arm. "It's getting frigid out here, and she's got people waiting for coffee."

That got Nikki's attention. Her breath caught. "The coffee beans!" She rushed back into the shop, the half empty arms of his coat swinging down by her knees as she jogged. Josh squeezed his eyes shut and took a moment to suck in and then release a slow breath. Deciding he was not calm enough to discuss his feelings, he clicked pause on their brewing argument. For now, at least.

"I'm going to walk the perimeter." Josh gestured to the alley. "Just to make sure it's secure."

Perry nodded. "We'll meet you inside, and we can have a chat." The marshal gestured to Agent Sterling to follow him inside.

Josh pushed the back door closed behind them and walked around the outside of the shop, in the direction Nikki had indicated. However, the only people Josh saw were townsfolk hurrying along the walkways in the center of town so they could get to their destination and get out of the cold.

A light snow was starting to fall. The snowflakes danced around the darkened streetlights and boxwood bushes, the only plants still green. Flurries pricked the bare skin of his arms. His eyes roamed over the quaint, idyllic store fronts, taking in the charm of Poppy's Pies, Quilting Dee's, and Bieler's Amish Kitchen. The chill had cooled his temper but it couldn't end the worry.

His hometown seemed like something out of a pleasant daydream. A place to put down roots and spend weekends watching old black and white films at the little one screen theater and summers on the amusement park's Ferris wheel where one could see the view of rolling hills and corn fields. It looked as if nothing bad could happen there but Josh knew better. He'd lost his previous wife to cancer in this town. *Lord, help me not lose Nikki too.*

***

Half of the ground coffee beans meant for the filter now speckled her front counter. Anxiety seemed to bring out the clumsy in her. Nikki pushed up the giant sleeves of Josh's coat and pulled a tea towel from the pocket of her apron and brushed the crumbs into a pile.

It killed her that Josh worried about her so much, but didn't he realize she worried about him too? Her parents had been criminals. They'd had a relationship of some kind with a ruthless villain. And Josh was getting dragged right into that world. True, going outside had been a risk, but didn't he understand how much she wanted to find her brother? She'd been alone her whole life. Had known almost nothing about her past and then suddenly a link had appeared out of nowhere. Did he expect her to just let that go? She had to see Rob again. To find out what type of man he was. And what about her parents? He was the only person in the world who could tell her stories of her life before they were killed. She had to find him.

And if she wouldn't abandon her brother, she wouldn't endanger her future husband either. And if that meant going off alone, how could Josh expect anything different? Her head was spinning from all the uncertainty. Maybe concentrating on the things she could control would be best. Starting with the mess she had made.

Eyeing the small trash can on a low shelf below the cash register, Nikki grabbed it. Holding the bin between her thigh and the counter, she used her towel to push the wasted grounds into the trash. She sat the bin on the floor and then wiped her forehead with the back of her hand when she caught sight of Josh lingering outside the store front windows.

The flurries had thickened, blurring the edges of his body as he stood on the sidewalk. Why wouldn't he come back inside? He must be freezing? After all, he hadn't even taken back his coat.

Should she take it out to him? She fingered the zipper against her neck. The coat had done the trick. She wasn't cold, but she couldn't seem to make herself take it off. She would've for him, though. At any moment, he could've come in and got it, and yet there he stood, scanning the area in full cop mode, looking for answers that just weren't there. Was that what she was doing too? All the emotions and hopes roiled around inside her, but she couldn't isolate what exactly she hoped to find.

She looked at Perry, Mike, and the FBI agent sitting at one of the dining tables. Would she get answers from them?

Would they help her find her family or were *they* the reason her brother was nowhere to be found?

"Er... Nikki?"

Nikki blinked and saw that Anna stood in front of her at the counter. "I'm sorry. I was lost in my thoughts. Did you need more coffee or another doughnut?"

"No." Anna's eyes darted around, and she held her book to her chest. "Could I talk to you for a second? Privately?"

Privately? How odd. What could she need to tell Nikki that everyone couldn't hear? "Why don't we go back to the kitchen?" Nikki motioned to the swinging double doors.

Anna nodded.

They pushed their way through the door. Once they reached the kitchen, Nikki turned. "What's up?"

She tucked a blonde strand behind her ear. "This is going to sound weird, but after you left the dining room, that one man in the suit seemed to follow you. Then, barely a minute later, another man came into the shop. He walked up to my table and told me to give you this." Anna set her book down on the stainless-steel island and opened the hard cover to reveal a picture. A photograph very similar to the one her brother had given her the night before. Nikki reached for it. It wasn't winter in this picture. They were at the beach. Her mom and dad lounged in reclined beach seats, their hands clasped across the gap between them. Nikki and Rob played in the sand at their feet. The image was different, but the emotion was the same: happiness. They looked happy.

Tears filled her eyes. So it *was* Rob outside, and she'd missed her chance to stop him. If Josh hadn't shown up, he might have given her the picture himself. Did he remember that day? Had her father held her on his shoulders and walked into the surf to get splashed by the waves? Did her mom give them wrapped peanut butter and jelly sandwiches out of a cooler she packed early that morning? Josh's arrival might have stolen a memory she never thought she would have.

Anna put a hand on her shoulder. "Sweetie, I didn't mean to upset you. Did I do the wrong thing by giving it to you? Do you want me to get Josh?"

"No." The word came out quickly. "I'm fine. Really." She wiped her cheek with the back of her hand. "You did good. Thank you for giving this to me. Did you see what the man looked like? Did Mike see him too?" She had to be sure it was him and not someone using the picture as a threat, taunting her with the fact that she could lose her brother forever.

Anna squeezed her eyes shut for a moment as if in thought. "I... I think Mike was taking his dishes to the rack on top of the garbage can. It all happened so fast I'd be surprised if he caught a look at him before he left. I think the man had dark hair based on his dark eyebrows, but he was wearing one of those winter hats with the flaps over the ears so I can't say for sure. He was tall. Medium build I think, but any more than that I really can't say. He was in and out. I'm sorry I don't have more."

Nikki's heart raced. Was there no way to be sure? She chided herself for never considering installing cameras outside for security. Frustrated tears filled her eyes. She wanted to be alone before they started spilling down her cheeks. "Don't be sorry at all. Thanks so much for giving me this."

Anna twirled a lock of her hair with a finger, glancing at the floor like she felt guilty for prying. "Do you know that man?"

Nikki shrugged, forcing down the knot in her throat. *Please Lord, help me keep it together.* "I think I used to. He's my brother." She slipped the picture into her apron's pocket and then closed the cover of the book and slid it across the shiny metal to Anna.

Anna laid a hand atop the volume, stopping its progress. "There's something else."

"What?"

"I noticed that something was written on the back." Her eyes were questioning. Not in an intrusive way but in an I-can't-help-you-if-you-don't-tell-me kind of way.

Nikki jammed her fingers back into her pocket and pulled out the picture. Flipping it over, she saw a message scrawled with a hurried hand. *They're the reason Mom and Dad are gone. Don't trust them. Wait for me.*

CHAPTER 10

THE DOORBELL CHIMED AS JOSH stepped inside the front door at Apple's. He spotted Perry and Mike with Agent Sterling at a corner table to his right. Perry waved to him and grabbed a nearby chair, dragging it over. Josh cringed as the leg scraped across Apple's hardwood floor. While he was grateful Perry was including him and seemed to be getting on with Mike, Josh had sanded and stained these floors himself in the rebuild and didn't want them to get scratched.

"I didn't see anyone outside." Josh dropped onto the chair and looked over his shoulder for Nikki but didn't see her. Maybe he should go find her and his coat. He pushed his fingers into his hair, shaking off some snowflakes.

Mike tapped a finger on the table. "Could be there was no one there."

Perry leaned back in his chair, crossing his arms behind his head. "We're gonna pretend it was someone. The question is, was it Rob looking for his sister; your rogue detective's mystery accomplice; Kent Marcus, the cop from his old precinct out for revenge; or the Snitch's people trying to tie up loose ends."

Josh glanced at Agent Sterling. There was no surprise in his face when Perry mentioned Rob or the Snitch. That must mean he knew who Nikki really was and why her brother was in WITSEC. Was that a good idea? In Josh's experience, the more people who knew a secret, the more likely it was to get out.

The agent turned to Josh, his eyes inquisitive. He must have sensed something in Josh's narrowed gaze because he cleared his throat. "Don't worry. The Snitch is officially the FBI's case and every agent has read the file at some point. I only just learned about the brother though. The marshals keep that kind of thing to themselves."

Josh wasn't convinced. "A lot of good that did him."

Perry wrinkled his nose as if he caught a bed smell. "You think someone found out where he was?"

Josh shrugged. "Why else would he run? Are you saying it's not possible that someone found out his location?"

Perry dropped his hands into his lap. "The marshals always have a plan in case someone finds out where we've set up a witness. But I'm just not sure. The truth is that we don't know what Rob is up to."

"That makes it sound like you think my brother is up to no good."

Mike's eyes widened in his periphery. Josh looked up at Nikki who had appeared at his side. Her tone was defensive. Her chin jutted out and she'd crossed her arms over her chest. She was swimming in his coat, but he was glad she hadn't taken it off. He hoped she felt close to him in it. Maybe felt comforted by his scent still on the fabric. The same way he felt giddy after a date when he smelled her perfume lingering in his truck.

Perry held up a hand like a crossing guard stopping a stampede of angry traffic. "I'm not saying that at all. I'm just saying we really can't say one way or another who broke into your house last night or why." He drained the rest of his coffee and set the cup down next to a trio of empty plates. Plates Nikki had likely filled for free.

They couldn't just keep sitting around eating Apple's profits in coffee and doughnuts as they waited for something to happen. "Then let's find out who it wasn't."

Perry gaped at him. "And how do you expect to do that?"

"We don't know who the Snitch is so we can't ask him. And we can't ask Rob anything because we can't find him. But... we can find out if the intruder came because of Vaughn."

His stomach churned at the memory of how close he and Nikki had come to losing their lives.

Nikki's hand fell onto his shoulder. "How can we find that out?"

Josh grinned up at her. "We go ask him. What do you think, marshal?"

"He is in a maximum-security prison for drug trafficking and murder."

Josh snorted. "Then I guess it's a good thing I have two federal officers here that can get me in to see him." This was the perfect opportunity. He glanced at the clock hanging above the door. 2:51 p.m. He was almost done with his shift.

The sound of a clearing throat sounded above him. He glanced up at his fiancée.

She straightened her stance. "That can get *us* in to see him."

Agent Sterling scoffed. "Yeah, why don't we just rent a bus and take the whole Podunk town with us?"

Mike whistled. "Podunk? Whoa, man."

What did Perry see in this guy? Josh clenched his teeth. He didn't want Nikki going either but some stranger wasn't going to order her around and insult his hometown. Josh opened his mouth to give the FBI agent a strong suggestion on what he could do with his attitude when Nikki cut in.

"Try and keep me from going." Josh heard her foot tapping next to him.

"Surrender, Luke." Josh wasn't surprised at Perry's directive. The marshal would know by now that Nikki could hold her own. "There's no arguing with her."

Agent Sterling glanced to Josh like he was looking for confirmation or pleading for help. The agent's eyes bounced between him and Nikki. His face saying something along the lines of *Are you going to let this happen?*

Josh raised an eyebrow, wondering if the other man had a girlfriend who he tried to order around like this. Probably not. A strong woman wouldn't give this guy the time of day. "Well, *I* certainly can't make her stay."

***

My toes are going to be frostbitten before we even get there. Nikki held her coat tight to stop the shivering and tucked her chin behind her wrapped scarf. Josh's coat was much warmer than hers, but she couldn't let him go out into the cold without it. Scooching forward in her seat, she reached out and turned the temperature control knob in Josh's patrol car to the next highest setting. Snow started falling in earnest as they got close to the maximum-security prison in neighboring Lane County and she just couldn't seem to get warm.

Josh looked over. "Are you still cold? I have blankets in the trunk. I could stop…"

"I don't want to stop. We'll lose the others. I know we're only going to be an hour outside of town but they're not local. What if they get lost?" She nodded to the brake lights flashing on and off in front of them. Perry and his FBI friend, Agent Sterling, were leading the caravan.

Josh glanced down towards his speedometer on the dashboard. "Considering how slow Agent Sterling is going, we could probably pull off the road go for a hike and come back and pull back out right behind him."

Out of towners were always the same. Nikki chuckled. The agent should've let Perry drive. "Don't get mad at him. He's a city guy. He's not used to driving on back roads that are barely big enough for one car let alone two and have turns so tight you can't see if someone's about to run right into you on the other side. And now they're covered in snow, which makes them even more treacherous." She wasn't worried though. At least, not about Josh's driving. She fully trusted in him to get them there safe.

It didn't seem like she'd changed his mind since Josh rolled his eyes. "He didn't seem to have any trouble with the roads when I pulled him over earlier."

Nikki held her hands over the heat coming out of the vents and smiled. "Maybe he's scared you're going to give him another ticket." After they'd left Apple's, Josh had told her how he and Agent Sterling came to meet. She doubted it would be a meeting the agent would soon forget.

Josh grabbed the lapel of his coat and started pulling it back over his shoulder. "Do you want my coat back?"

She remembered the way he'd wrapped her in it when they were outside her shop, and she wished the smells embedded into the threads were still sending reminders of her fiancé up where she could breathe them in. But it would be selfish to ask for it. How else would he stay warm? "No. I'm really fine. I don't even think I'm cold. I think it's more nerves."

Josh put a hand on her knee. "Vaughn won't be able to hurt you, you know. He'll be shackled when we see him. He won't be able to do anything."

"I'm not worried of what he's going to do. I'm worried about what he is going to say." Or not say. She tugged on the loose hair hanging down the side of her face.

"Anything we get from him will be more than we have now."

But what if he says something I don't want to hear? So far, her brother had warned her not to trust Josh, the man she desperately loved, and then told her not to trust the marshals or the FBI. Was she going to be the only one in the interview room that *didn't* have a terrible secret to hide?

She sighed. "I guess, I wish we were talking to him by ourselves."

"Without Perry and Agent Sterling, we wouldn't be able to get in at all. Prisons don't exactly like surprises and they certainly won't drag out one of their more dangerous inmates at the request of a sheriff's deputy from another county."

"I know but…" She stopped herself. She was about to say she didn't know if she could trust them when she realized she wasn't one hundred percent sure she could trust him either. But she wanted too.

89

"But…" Josh raised an eyebrow.

Nikki shook her head. "Nothing. Just… er what if he won't talk in front of them?"

The car slowed around a turn. Josh leaned forward, looking out the windshield. "Well, we're about to find out. We're here."

Nikki squinted, trying to make out the building through the snow fall thickening every second.

Their car crept along a thin road. In the distance, Nikki caught sight of a tall chain link fence. Nikki leaned her head against the side window and looked out at the barbed wire coils looping through the top links of the tall fence.

She didn't like being there but who did? Their route led them to a portion of the fence that had tall towers on each side of the road. Nikki saw men through glassless windows at the tops and two more men standing outside the fence near the gate. Agent Sterling pulled to a stop. The guards approached the agent's window.

Nikki leaned forward in her seat and squinted through the snow-spattered windshield, wishing she could read lips. "Do you think they will turn us away?"

Josh rubbed the palm of his right hand across the top of the steering wheel. "Two Federal officers? No way."

Nikki grabbed the arm rest on her door. "But look, they're going back to the gate. They're not going to open it." To have come so far only to be turned away would be the worst.

Josh gripped the wheel and tilted his head to the side. "They took their IDs. They're just confirming they are who they say they are."

What if he was wrong or this turned out to be some sort of crazy setup? Would they end up being the ones behind bars? After a few minutes, a red light hanging on the fence turned from red to green and a loud screeching sound pierced her ears as the gate started to open. A loud siren blew for a moment and then stopped when the gate was fully opened.

The SUV's brake lights went from red to black, and they started moving forward. Josh followed, nodding to the guards as they passed.

Nikki let out a breath and relaxed back into her seat.

Josh nudged her leg and smirked. "Don't count your chickens yet. That was the easy part."

CHAPTER 11

NIKKI'S SKIN WAS PALE AND blotchy with worry by the time they got into the interview room. Josh had only been half serious when he'd said getting into the prison was the easy part but his words ended up being a premonition of what actually happened. It took every bit of weight Agent Sterling and Perry had to get them in this room, and it looked like it was the last place Nikki wanted to be. But who would like being in this room? The harsh florescent lights glinted off the steel table, and Josh noticed the black shadows of dead flies inside their cover. The tinting on the two way mirror made them all look haggard. Their eyes wrapped in dark circles.

This was not a room made for this many people. Even though he'd spent time in foxholes in the army, Josh felt cramped. His fiancée looked like she was about to burst.

She sat next to him, her knee bouncing up and down under the metal table and her hands wringing in her lap. Josh laid a hand on her shoulder. She turned to him and he gave what he hoped was a reassuring smile.

Perry and Agent Sterling pulled chairs up to the ends of the table. Both of them sat casually and stone-faced like conversing with criminals was an everyday event for them. Josh fixed his eyes on the empty chair across the table from him. The chair reserved for a murderer. A former colleague. A supposed friend.

The sound of a dragging chain drew Josh's eyes to the metal mesh-filled glass window in the door. Nikki's lithe muscles tensed under his palm. A guard standing at least six foot five inches with muscles nearly busting through the fabric of his uniform pushed open the door and ushered Vaughn Grimes into the room.

Vaughn stopped in the doorway, freezing the minute his eyes met Josh's. "I don't have anything to say to these people."

The guard wrapped an enormous hand around his arm. "Then don't talk."

Vaughn looked over his shoulder down the hall and then back to the guard staring daggers. Was he deciding whether he was going to be difficult?

Josh checked the guard for a reaction. No way would he pick a fight with a guy that size. After a moment, Vaughn jerked out of the guard's grasp but instead of trying to push out the door, he slowly made his way to the empty chair, the shackles stretching from his hands to his ankles clanking with every step.

"This is going to be a dull conversation." Vaughn growled as he plopped down into the seat.

Perry shifted in his chair. "We've got time to wait."

Vaughn snorted as the guard grabbed the cuffs around his wrists and lifted them onto the table. "So do I and it's much nicer in here than in my cell."

That's sure saying something. The guard locked the wrist cuffs to a metal loop sticking out of the middle of the steel table. "I'll be right outside the door." The guard glanced at Josh, giving him a you're-from-around-here nod of solidarity. "Just yell when you're done."

"Got it. Thanks." *Here we go. Lord, give me the right words to say.*

Vaughn tapped his fingers on the table, his eyes locked on Josh, a sly smile painted on his face.

Nothing Vaughn could do would intimidate him. Josh leaned back in his chair and let the tips of his fingers trace circles on Nikki's shoulders. He knew how to wait out a suspect. Vaughn would get frustrated sooner or later and slip up and then Josh would make a move.

"Do you know why we are here, Mr. Grimes?" Agent Sterling asked.

"I'm guessing you need something." He turned his insidious expression to Nikki. "But I'm not exactly in a giving mood."

Josh wished he could order Vaughn to keep his eyes off her but he'd lose the upper hand if he let his emotions get the best of him.

Perry cleared his throat. "Maybe we're just here to add another crime to your already long list of offenses."

Vaughn let out a laugh as he turned to the marshal. "And when would I have been able to commit this supposed crime? They don't exactly give day passes here."

Josh let go of Nikki and crossed his fingers on the tabletop. "You know as well as anyone that crimes are ordered from prison all the time."

Vaughn's head tilted to the side, and his mouth split into a wicked smile. "And what is it you think I ordered, Deputy Bennet?"

Josh narrowed his gaze. He thought over last night's events. Abigail's injuries. Nikki being dragged across her basement floor. "We'll start with attempted kidnapping but you can add assault to that as well."

Vaughn's eyes flashed to Nikki. "She doesn't *look* like someone tried to kill her."

"Why do you assume it was me?" Nikki's expression was cold and unaffected. A few minutes ago, she seemed ready to burst, but now she seemed completely at ease. Josh would've been surprised at the transformation if he didn't already know that she'd probably learned how to keep her cool around violent men because she'd been around them her whole life. A fact that broke his heart and renewed his internal commitment to show her what true love was like.

The prisoner rolled his eyes. "Why else would your bodyguard be here if not to keep his damsel out of distress?"

"But you…" Nikki crossed her arms. "You would love it if I was in distress. After all, you're only in here because of me. In fact, you'd probably do anything to get revenge. Even send someone after me, telling them to take out anyone who got in their way."

Vaughn raised his hand like he wanted to touch his face or maybe scratch his chin as he considered Nikki's words, but he was stopped short by the chain hooked to the table. He groaned.

"Oops." Perry's face reflected in the glass split into a smile.

Vaughn glared at the marshal for a moment and then turned his attention back to Nikki, his eyes cold and unfeeling. "If I had sent someone after you, I wouldn't have sent them to take you. I would've sent them to kill you. And it turns out, I don't need to send them." The side of his mouth curled up in a satisfied smirk. "Someone a lot worse than me is after you."

Bingo. Josh straightened in his chair. "And who would that be?" He leaned forward onto his elbows, feeling a rush of inspiration. "The same person who helped you try to kill us? The woman that made the phony 911 call? Or maybe the monster you referred to while you held us a gunpoint? The one some people call the Snitch?"

"If you know, why are you here?" Vaughn raised an eyebrow. "Hoping you're wrong? You're right to be scared."

Josh glanced at Agent Sterling. He was trying to look unaffected but Josh saw a twitch of excitement in his eyes. At last, they were getting somewhere. And no doubt the agent was probably thinking about the promotion he'll get if he was the one to bring down the Snitch.

"I never said I was scared." Nikki's tone sounded amused but Josh knew it was a facade.

Vaughn glanced around the table. "You should be. You have enemies all around you."

Nikki's skin went white. Her breath caught. The prisoner's words had struck a chord, but why? Did she know something he didn't?

She uncrossed her arms and squeezed her fingers together against her thigh like she was trying to keep them from shaking.

Enough with the veiled threats. "Maybe you should be the one who's scared. Don't you think so, Perry?"

The marshal turned to him with a crinkled brow but then his expression brightened as he caught on. "Yes. I know I'd be scared if I were you, Vaughn."

"And why's that?"

Agent Sterling scooted his chair closer to the table. "Think about it, man. The Snitch may be after Ms. Appleton for some crazy reason but we'll protect her. Who's going to protect you?"

Vaughn grunted. "I don't need protecting. I'm on his side."

"We know that." Josh smiled. "But does he?"

Vaughn straightened in his chair and cleared his throat. "Why wouldn't he?"

Josh scratched the stubble on his chin and began to spin a plausible story, hoping the man would take the bait. "Think about it for a second. He helped you in your plan to frame her and when that didn't work, kill her. He probably was happy for you to kill the daughter of the former associates that tried to frame him but… you failed. And now you're here. Talking to *us*."

Vaughn scowled. "But I haven't told you anything."

"How would he know that?" Agent Sterling gestured with his hands, indicating the lack of cameras and listening devices in this tiny room.

"If he's watching—and I have a feeling he is—all he's going to know is that you met with the FBI and the US Marshals." Josh tapped his chin with a finger. "Someone as protective of his identity as he is probably tends to assume the worst. Which in this case would be that you talked? How long do you think it will take someone like that to get to him in here, Perry?"

The marshal shrugged. "I doubt he has more than a day."

Vaughn's eyes went wide, and he started to squirm in his chair, his ankles chains jingling as he moved. Was he considering his options? He didn't look optimistic. He looked scared. "He won't come after me. He knows I don't know anything about him. If there is nothing I can tell you, then there is no reason to kill me." Josh thought the words were true but Vaughn's confidence from before had left, making his voice soft and almost childlike.

"Maybe." Agent Sterling shrugged. "But he doesn't seem like the kind of guy to take that risk. Careful as he is, I think he'd rather be safe than sorry. Could be that he figures that if you're alive you probably won't talk but if you're dead, you *definitely* won't talk."

"I-I..." Vaughn balled his hands into fists on the table and tugged against the chain. "I don't have anything I can tell you."

Josh snorted. "Do you honestly expect me to believe that. To believe that you—a trained law enforcement officer—worked with them on more than one occasion and didn't learn a single thing." Josh pointed a finger in his face. "We never found the black sedan that ran Nikki off the road or the woman who made the 911 call to frame Nikki. The Snitch gave you someone to help you craft your scheme. After all that planning, you are seriously trying to say that you don't know a single thing about your accomplice or her boss?"

Vaughn opened his mouth like he was going to respond but then closed it. He squeezed his eyes closed and shook his head.

"Have it your way, man." Perry pushed his chair back, the legs scraping on the floor. "You're on your own. When the Snitch's assassin comes, give him a message. Tell him we're coming for him."

Josh followed the marshal's lead, rising to his feet. Grabbing the jacket on the back of Nikki's chair, he waited until she got to her feet and then held it up for her to slip her arms into the sleeves. Agent Sterling jumped up and knocked on the door to the interrogation room. "Guard."

"Wait." Vaughn slammed his shackles onto the table. "Just wait, okay!"

The locks released and the door opened. The same burly guard poked his head through. "You guys done with him?"

Agent Sterling turned to Perry. "What do you think? We done with him?"

Perry stroked his chin. "Looks like we need one more minute. If you don't mind."

"You got it." The door closed again, and the locks clicked into place.

They got him. Josh fought back a smile.

"Look, you guys got to protect me." Vaughn's eyes pleaded for mercy.

Josh fixed his stare on him. "First, give us something we can use."

***

Nikki braced her hands on the counter and tried to breathe, but her wrecked nerves and the strong smell of disinfectant that was heavy in the guard station's bathroom only seemed to make it worse. She looked up into the mirror. The florescent lights brought out the dark circles under her bloodshot eyes. She'd had to get out of the interrogation room. She couldn't listen to it anymore. What Vaughn had said…

Please Lord, it can't be.

If what he said wasn't just an attempt to scare her, what did it mean for everything she'd come to hold dear? Had her whole life in St. Claire been a lie? *You always knew it was too good to be true.* Did she? Was she deluding herself with this faith stuff too? Had she ignored reality? Josh had shown her a whole new way of living. He had helped her find God, but what if he was just telling her what she wanted to hear? What if love, grace, and forgiveness weren't for someone like her? What if they weren't real at all? How could she go back to living without them?

Nikki heard a soft knock at the door. "Nikki? Honey, are you in there?"

"Be right out." She turned her back to the mirror. It wasn't a good view. Josh would totally see something was wrong if she didn't do something. Nikki smacked on the faucet and splashed cold water into her face. Eyes closed, she felt for the paper towel dispenser. After dabbing her face dry, she smoothed back her hair, tucking it behind her ears. She wrapped her emerald scarf around her neck, grabbed her purse off the counter, and took another look. It wasn't that much of an improvement but there was no time to do anything else. Her hands were shaking when she pulled open the bathroom door, so she stuffed them into the pockets of her coat.

"Ready to go?" Josh brushed his hand across the small of her back.

"Yep." She nodded.

Josh ushered her over to the metal detectors. She let her bag fall off her shoulder and into the basket on the conveyor

100

belt. "What about Agent Sterling and Perry?" She glanced around for the other men.

A prison guard motioned her through the partitions.

"They have to stay." Josh followed her through. He reached into the basket rolling out of the x-ray machine and grabbed his wallet, keys, and her purse. "The guards moved him to solitary confinement to keep him away from the other inmates. Perry's going to arrange for him to be transported to another facility. They'll accept him under a different name until they make further plans. Perry and Agent Sterling are going to meet us back home once they finish making their arrangements."

Nikki grabbed her purse when he held it out to her and slung the strap over her shoulder. "I don't know if I like this. What if they let him go free?"

Josh grabbed her hand and raised it to his cheek. He brushed her knuckles across his stubble. "They won't. He would have to do something or reveal information that would guarantee an arrest and conviction. What we just heard wasn't that."

Josh dropped their intertwined hands down to his waist and started leading Nikki to the imposing exit doors. Nikki chewed her lip as she fell in step beside him. Josh had lived his whole life in St. Claire. He shouldn't be so calm. How could he not be as shocked as her? Was he putting on a brave face? Or was he fine because this was information he already knew?

Vaughn had stared at the table while he let it spill. "I didn't find out that Nikki had ended up in St. Claire on my own. After her ex got put away, I planned on finishing her off once things had cooled off a bit."

Nikki had watched Josh's hands squeeze into fists at the convict's words.

"But when I went to find her, she had already left town, and I had no way to find her. Then, months later I got a call saying where she was and what they wanted me to do. It was a woman. She said she was calling on behalf of the man called the Snitch. He wanted her set up. Discredited for some reason. So, I got myself a job down here so I could hatch a plan."

"How does this help us at all?" Josh smacked the table. "We need an ID."

Vaughn glowered at him. "I'm not finished. I heard something in the background during the call. At the time, I didn't know what it was, but after living in St. Claire for a while, I figured it out. It was the animatronic cowboy from the sharpshooter stand at that old amusement park just out of town."

Josh scoffed.

Nikki decided to say the thing he was most likely thinking. "So, what if they were here in town? If they were following me, they would be."

Vaughn rolled his eyes. "Someone said 'Hi' to her in the background. I'm pretty sure they called her by name but it was muffled. They must've covered the receiver to keep me from hearing, and then the phone went dead."

Nikki had frowned. "What is that supposed to mean?"

Perry sighed. "It means whoever she is, she lives St. Claire and is probably not alone. Crime is organizational. There's no way there's one lone criminal out here working for the Snitch."

Frigid wind hit her face, bringing her back. Nikki shivered. Josh wrapped an arm around her shoulders and pulled her close. The snow was still falling and had gotten worse since they'd arrived. Nikki couldn't see more than a few feet in front of her and her foot slipped on an icy patch.

Josh squeezed, steadying her so she didn't slip farther. She wobbled but then stood straight. "Pennsylvania." He chuckled, shaking snowflakes off his golden hair. "One of the only states where you get all four seasons in a matter of days. Tomorrow we'll probably be sweating."

Nikki let out a breath as they reached Josh's patrol car. "Well, I'd like to skip this season, I think. Do you think we'll get home okay?"

Josh brushed the snow away from the passenger side door handle and then pulled it open. The white covering on top, disturbed by the action, came down like a white waterfall onto the concrete parking lot. "This thing's all-wheel-drive. No worries."

Nikki batted at some snow that had fallen onto the seat with her hand and then climbed into the vehicle. "If you say so."

But all she had were worries. Someone close to the Snitch lived in her town. Meaning other people living there might be on his payroll, too.

Even Josh.

CHAPTER 12

JOSH SQUINTED, LOOKING FOR GLIMPSES of other cars through the whiteout conditions. He wasn't scared to drive in snow but it would be foolish not to be extra cautious. They were getting close to St. Claire, and Nikki had been silent the whole ride, leaving him serenaded by the blowing heater, swishing wiper blades, rumbling engine, and crunch of fallen snow being ground into the asphalt and gravel by his tires.

Branches on the tree lined road sagged under the weight of it and would sometimes give out, dropping white snowballs onto the windshield as they made their way on the winding roads back to St. Claire.

A weirdness crawled over his skin. These trees. These roads. He'd seen them all before. Took them is whole life, and yet now they seemed unfamiliar to him. His world had turned strange. St. Claire was supposed to be idyllic, peaceful, serene. But now it was tainted.

Why am I so surprised? Josh had been near evil before. He'd seen the aftermath of terrible crimes. And he'd been to war. But wasn't home supposed to be different? He wasn't naïve. The people of St. Claire were struggling against the spread of drug addiction, but he took for granted that its people were generally good. That Vaughn's actions had been an anomaly. That he'd brought the trouble to Josh's hometown instead of finding it there. How could people working for a monster like the Snitch be hidden among the faces he'd grown up seeing? And why did they choose to set up here?

Nikki's voice broke into his thoughts. "What are you thinking about?"

Josh glanced at Nikki in the passenger seat. Dark circles hugged her lower lids and her already fair complexion looked gray as the sky outside. He needed a sounding board and given her reaction to Vaughn's implication that she was surrounded by enemies, he was going to be as transparent as possible.

The back windshield still looked like a sheet of ice in the rearview mirror. He reached out and pressed the button to turn up the rear defroster.

"He said the woman on the phone named the Snitch specifically. Meaning, she wasn't just a random drug dealer he was using and then cutting loose because from what Perry said, they never knew the real identity of who they were working with. This person must actually be close to him because after all this time, he wouldn't let just anyone into his circle of trust."

"So..."

"So that makes me think there is a relationship there." A peace settled in his chest. This felt right, like the fog was starting to clear.

Nikki shifted in her seat. "Maybe a significant other?"

Josh ran his tongue across his front teeth. "Hmmm... Maybe but relationships like that end all the time. I'm thinking more along the lines of family. He's been running this game for decades. Family would provide a consistency to make that feasible. I'm thinking a sister or maybe a daughter."

She twisted towards him. "You think he really cares about this person?"

"What other reason could he have for having his posse set up here in St. Claire? Yes, we have a drug problem, but being closer to a city would provide access to a much bigger market for a criminal organization. Maybe he stashed this mystery woman here to keep her safe."

"Or the mystery woman and her associates just saw this as a good place to hide." Nikki shifted towards him in her seat. "I mean, that's why *I* came here. To hide. They could be commuting to take care of their business and then coming back here. And who knows how many there are? These people could be passing me on the street every day. They could be... anyone."

Josh glanced at her again. There was something off about her. She'd been different since the moment Rob walked into their lives. She had her arms tight around her and her shoulders were slumped like she was trying to make herself smaller. She scooted close to her door. Almost like she didn't want to be near him. She couldn't possibly think *he* was the—

"Look out!" Nikki's eyes went wide, and her hands flew up to the dash to brace herself.

Josh turned back to the road. A large SUV lay on its side stretched across their lane and was consumed by a roaring fire.

Stopping was pointless. In these road conditions, slamming on the brakes would send them sliding right into the flames and metal. Josh jerked the wheel to the left, praying they could get around the wreckage. The front of the patrol car swung around the bumper of the burning vehicle, and Josh felt the back tire catch the lip of the road. They were going to end up in the steep ditch. What if he flipped it?

He turned the wheel back to the right and floored it. The car bumped back onto the road barely avoiding the flaming SUV, but the roads were too slick and they went into a spin.

Jesus, help us!

The back of the patrol car swung towards the ditch on the other side of the road. Josh turned into the skid, hoping to course correct, but as the car spun back the other way, the front tires hit another patch of ice. Josh's whole body lifted off the seat as the front of the car flew over the edge and came down hard on the other side. A hulking tree seemed to come out of nowhere, and Josh spun the wheel to the right but then lost his grip. The driver's side fender crunched into the trunk.

Light flashed in his head like fireworks and then everything went black.

A smell like gun powder brought him back to consciousness. The air blurred with white powder. Josh pushed at the white pillowy thing in front of him. Was it the deflating air bag? His eyes fluttered closed and the black threatened to return.

"N-Nikki." Josh coughed. He tried to blink away the urge to sleep but his eyelids felt like anvils. He reached out a hand, letting it flop around feeling for his fiancée. "It's okay, honey." His fingers found skin. He found her hand and held it tight, but it was limp in his grasp. "Talk to me, baby."

He begged the darkness to go away. They needed help. He needed to call for help. *Lord, help me stay awake.* He let his

107

hand trail up her palm to her wrist, pressing down to find a pulse but just when he felt a beat, her arm was jerked away.

Josh opened his eyes. His head throbbed. The open-doorbell started dinging from the dash, and a gust of frigid air pummeled him. There was a man. He pushed the door open. Josh squinted at him. He knew the man. He was sure of it. But... what was his name?

Nikki moved farther away from him, her body flailing as the man dragged her over the door frame. Her eyes were closed. She wasn't fighting him.

"No!" Josh called out.

He tried to launch himself over the middle console, howling in pain. The muscles down his neck screamed for relief. He had to grab her. To stop her from being taken. But the seatbelt pulled tight across his chest, holding him in place. Bits of broken glass red with blood from cuts up his arm clinked together as he fumbled for the latch and pushed the release. He pulled his door handle and leaned against it, but it was stuck. The tree had obliterated his side mirror. The damage must have jammed the door.

Josh turned back to Nikki. She was out of the car now. Her figure was shrinking into the snow. The man picked her up. He swung her over his shoulder and looked at Josh before turning away. Josh gasped. Rob. Her brother was taking her away.

Clawing at the empty seat, Josh pulled until he thought his biceps would rip apart. He didn't have enough leverage to hoist himself up, so he twisted back towards his door. Josh threw his whole body against his door. It let out a wrenching sound and then swung open. Josh fell out onto the snow like a bag of rocks. The slush swallowed his hands as he pushed himself to his feet. He took a step, and the ground went out from under him as his feet slid down the steep side of the ditch. And with one swoop, he was on his back, the wind knocked out of him. He gasped and rolled to his side and then up on his hands and knees as he fought to regain his breath. He pushed himself to his feet and staggered to the tree he'd hit. He peered into the trees, trying to see where Rob had taken Nikki, but he saw only white. They were gone... *She* was gone.

***

"Rob?" Nikki pushed herself upright in the back seat of a strange car and stared into the rearview mirror's reflection of her brother. Her chest felt like someone was sitting on it and the muscles down her neck and into her back hurt at the slightest movement. "W-Where are we going?"

His eyes flashed on her. "Somewhere safe."

This wasn't right. Something was missing. She held her fingers over her closed eyelids, breathing through the pain of the headache behind her eyes. What had happened? She remembered the SUV. The fire. The wreck.

"Josh! Wait, we have to get Josh. He's in the car. We went off the road and hit a tree."

Rob's eyes dropped out of view. "We're not going back for him."

"But he's my fiancé." Nikki spun around, wincing as she looked out the back windshield for the wreck but all she saw was white. How long had it been? She looked down at her chest. Fresh snow was caked in the creases of her jacket. They were still close. "I love him. Turn around!"

Rob grunted. "He's a liar. He would have taken you right to the Snitch."

Nikki grabbed the back of his seat and swallowed the acid bubbling in the back of her throat. She couldn't breathe. Reaching up, she tore her scarf from around her neck. "That's not true. He loves me. He's been protecting me for months."

Rob squeezed the steering wheel. "More like keeping tabs on you."

"What are you talking about?" How could she think straight when the world wouldn't stop spinning? "We need to go back."

"It didn't take long for the Snitch to figure out that I escaped that car accident. They know I'm alive. He has been watching ever since in case I ever surfaced. He would rather have killed me, but he couldn't find me. But if he ever did, he'd have you as collateral to keep me from talking to the cops. Until a couple days ago, when I found out that someone in the marshal's service had tipped him off. I noticed someone had gone through Mom and Dad's stuff I had stored in my attic."

She clutched the edge of her seat. "You have stuff from Mom and Dad?"

He nodded and then kept talking. "If it had been the Snitch, I'd be dead already and the marshals are the only ones who know where I live. It had to be them. I had no way to know who was on my side or who wanted to sell me out. So, I took off and came for you but your boyfriend was always in my way, keeping you from me."

None of this made sense. Was she hearing him right? She caught sight of his eyes in the rearview mirror. They were quizzical and nervous.

"I tried to tell you the night we met. I didn't think you would believe me but I had to try. That's why I left you the note. If I ever remembered who he was, they knew having you would keep me silent."

Nikki rubbed her temples. She couldn't make his words stay. They kept drifting away like dreams did upon waking. All she could think about was Josh. Was he hurt? Who would help him like Rob helped her? "But… wait a minute. How did you find me so fast? How did you know where I would be? You couldn't predict the accident…"

Nikki scooted across the seat and splayed her fingers out on the window. Squinting through the gap between her hands, she looked outside. It was almost completely dark. What time had they left the prison? She remembered closing her shop and the long drive, but after that, things were fuzzy. The winding road looked familiar to her and she spotted an abandoned coal belt. They were definitely in Nadine. Maybe even close to St. Claire.

"I only found you so fast because I was in the SUV you almost hit." He started digging around in a bag on the passenger seat.

What was this road called? It was on the tip of her tongue. "B-but it was on fire."

Plastic crinkled and she turned back. Rob reached back holding a bottle of water out to her. "You should drink this."

She looked at it for a moment, her brain slow to grasp what it was. Then her thirst hit her. She *did* want something to drink. She snatched the bottle from her brother and

111

gulped it down. Water dripped down the sides of her mouth.

"My marshal had tracked me down. I told him what I knew, and he believed me when I told him someone else in the marshals was bad news. He agreed to take me to you. We were on our way to the prison to get you. Neal wanted to put you in a safe house with me while he sniffed out the mole in the department."

Rob cleared his throat. "Are you feeling okay? You should lie down on the seat. You need to rest"

Nikki held up a hand. "No. I'm fine. What happened then? Where is the marshal who found you?

"He, uh… didn't make it. We were driving, and then this car came flying up behind us. Neal, my marshal, sensed that whoever was chasing us was up to no good. But when they started firing on us, one of the tires blew." His voice cracked. "He pulled off the road, and we positioned ourselves in front of the car so we could get on the offensive. Neal told me to run and that he would hold them off. I didn't want to leave him there. I wanted to help, but he reminded me that if I died, who would protect you. I-I had to come for you. You're my only family. When I got far enough away, I stole this car and went back for him. The other car was gone but the SUV was on fire. Then I saw what was left of Neal inside it… burning too. I couldn't save him. Then some crazy stroke of luck sent you my way. I couldn't stop what happened to Neal but I *could* save you."

Images of burning flesh filled her mind. Only monsters would do that to a man, and her brother believed Josh was cut from the same cloth? Josh who prayed by her bedside that God would heal her? "I-I'm sorry. But I just don't think

Josh is part of… " Nikki tried to focus. What should they do next? How could she find out the truth about her future husband? Where should they hide? She had nothing. Everything was foggy now, and fatigue rushed over her. Was this the adrenaline wearing off after the accident or something else? She didn't know, but she couldn't fight it. She had to sleep. Nikki stretched out across the bench seat and let her eyes close.

CHAPTER 13

"REALLY, KOBY, I'M FINE." JOSH noticed Perry walking along the snow covered road in his direction. His form was lit up by all the flashing lights of the small army of emergency vehicles glowing like a lighthouse in the night. "I just wanted to call and see if you could watch Nikki's house in case she shows up there for some reason. It will only be for a little bit until Brandon can relieve you."

"Whatever you need."

"All right, I have to go. I'm glad you got a new phone so soon. I'll check in again in a bit. See you later man and... thank you."

"Why would Rob take her?" Perry swatted at some black ash lit up by the beam of a flashlight in a passing EMT's hand. It fluttered in front of his face like dust in the sunshine.

"I don't know. But it was definitely him." Josh removed the ball of gauze taped to his forehead to check if the wound was still bleeding and then turned to his mangled vehicle right next to him and kicked the rear tire. "I need another vehicle so I can find her."

Perry sucked a breath through his teeth. "I don't think you should be driving. You've barely let the EMTs touch you."

Josh glanced over the frenzied scribbles of tire tracks at the ambulance pulled off the side of the road. The back doors were open and Tuck sat inside. They had come after

Josh had called in the wreck and Nikki's kidnapping. "Because I'm fine." Other than the splitting headache, stinging gashes, and stiff muscles. But what if Nikki wasn't as lucky as him? She might need medical attention. *Lord, stay with her. Heal and keep her safe until I find her.*

"Clearly." Agent Sterling rolled his eyes as he stepped into the conversation, cheeks red from standing near the burning vehicle. "The fire's almost out. The city police are getting ready to move the vehicle off the road for safety."

Josh nodded. "The fire and snow probably destroyed most of the evidence anyway. I could tell it had been burning for a while when we got here. Even if I hadn't wrecked, I still wouldn't have made it in time to save the driver. It was engulfed. As soon as I freed myself, I ran over there and I saw... it was too late. He'd been gone for a while." Josh said a silent prayer for whoever had been in that SUV.

Agent Sterling nodded to the smoking heap of metal, his eyes changing colors in the flashing lights of the fire truck. "When I can get to it, I'll see if there's anything not turned to ash in the glove box to get an ID. The license plate is badly burned but I think it's a government tag. Maybe Justice Department?"

"It is." Perry sighed.

Josh jerked his head towards the marshal, causing him to wince as the sudden movement sent a shock down the stiff and sore muscles of his neck. "How do you know that?"

"Because I'm pretty sure I know who is in there." Perry frowned. "I think it's Neal Boggs, the marshal in charge of Rob's case."

Agent Sterling gaped.

Josh let his mind go to work. Pacing closer to the smoldering vehicle, Josh inspected it for clues. What did he expect to find? Maybe bullet holes? It was now just a burnt heap of metal. This was no accident. He knew it in his gut. This was murder.

He scanned the ground for footprints, hoping he'd find just one that hadn't been filled with snow. He had a sinking feeling. The first people cops questioned in a murder were the ones at the scene, and the only person Josh had seen was... But could he really accuse Nikki's brother of murder? "Rob could've done this."

Perry stroked the point of his chin. "I guess. But why? For what I know of him, Rob is a good guy. Sharp as a tack but not a killer."

"His parents *were* criminals." Agent Sterling's tone was excited like he *wanted* Nikki's brother to be the bad guy.

Perry must've noticed because he gave his shoulder a push. "What does that matter? He was just a kid."

Agent Sterling shrugged. "Hey, I was shoplifting at eight."

Was he serious? Would he really write off a child as a criminal because of who their parents were?

Perry crossed his arms over his chest. "And yet you became an FBI agent. I don't think that fact helps your argument any. Obviously, something is going on with Rob that we don't know about. Why would he leave witness protection in the first place? And why would he have run when we showed up at Nikki's last night? I-I hate to say this—especially considering where we're standing—but what if Neal was not who he seemed?"

If that was the case, Josh would feel better about Nikki being with Rob no matter how unwise his actions were today. They needed to be sure though. "We need information. The sheriff has all our deputies out searching for Rob and Nikki. Let's go back to the sheriff's station. You guys can use the conference room as a temporary headquarters. Only I want in on the investigation. We need to look at everything. If we search Rob's file, Vaughn's associates and the Snitch files, we might find possible locations Rob would hide out at and reasons why as well. People only run for two reasons. Because they're in danger or because they've committed a crime. Let's find out which one it is. Either way, Nikki's in danger."

Perry nodded. A grumbling sound grew louder. The tow truck was pushing through the gaps between vehicles. Josh motioned to the others to step off to the side and give it a wide birth.

The sooner they got started the sooner he could get Nikki back. Dread filled him. A sense that he was missing something. What are the chances the marshal would meet his end on the very road they were taking away from the prison?

"Hey, where did you guys end up putting Vaughn? Because I think we need to talk to him again. After all your friend was heading towards the prison when things went south. The only connection there to all this is Vaughn."

"We haven't put him anywhere yet." Perry brushed snow off his shins. "We got the call about your wreck and came right over."

117

Was he kidding? He left him at the prison? "What were you thinking? He can't go back to general population with the other inmates. Someone will get to him."

Agent Sterling reached into his pocket and pulled out a set of keys. "Relax. He's been separated and is under the direct supervision of the warden. He can sit tight while we head back to town."

Perry pushed back his shoulders like he was trying to stretch out a kink in his back. "And he won't be sitting long. Abigail is on her way to get him now. The hospital cleared her for active duty, so she's picking him up and taking him to one of our safe houses." Then he turned to Agent Sterling and held out a hand. "And since we don't want to grow old while you learn to drive in the snow, I'll take the keys."

Agent Sterling rolled his eyes but tossed them at the marshal.

Josh didn't like it, but what could he do? "Then I want to meet them there and take him back to the sheriff's station with us. I want him where I can watch him."

Perry put a hand on Josh's chest. "We don't let civilians know the location of government safe houses. That's not protocol."

Josh stuck out his chin. "He'd still be in your custody. You guys are still in charge. But until Nikki is home safe, we need to circle the wagons. I can work with you guys or I can try and find her on my own. So can we at least get started?" *Lord, don't let me get shut out.*

Perry's lips puckered as he tilted his head. "Well, you sure aren't driving that heap away." He dropped his hand and nodded to Josh's wrecked car. "So, I guess since you're going to be with us anyway, you might as well make yourself useful. We'll hit the safe house and then head back to St. Claire."

Josh nodded and followed them towards the blue rental parked opposite the fire truck when Mike grabbed his arm.

"Hey, got a sec?"

The others were still wading through the snow. "What's up?"

Mike eyed the agents as they walked away. "The sheriff asked if we'd help get the vehicles cleared. I rode here with the tow truck. As soon as we move the burnt one off to the side, we'll wait for the federal guys to pick it up and take it to their Pittsburgh offices for their crime scene techs. Then we're going to get your patrol car and tow it back to St. Claire."

"Awesome. Thanks for helping, man."

Mike waved him off. "No problem. The reason I stopped you is that while I was in town getting the truck, Anna showed up at the city garage looking for me. She wanted me to get a message to you that she needed to talk to you."

He pictured the young woman who always seemed to be carrying a book. Even today he'd seen her reading one at Apple's. What could she want with him? "Did she say why?"

"She'd just heard about Nikki disappearing from my brother, Brandon, as he was walking out of the sheriff's office. She said she needed to tell you something about Nikki's brother? I didn't even know she had a brother."

That had certainly come out of left field. What did a local baker have to do with his fiancée's mystery brother who—until a few days ago—had been in the witness protection program? "Um… okay. I have to go with the agents over there for a little bit but then we are going to the sheriff's station. Can you get a message to her telling her to be there in an hour or so? That will give me time for my detour and time to get back without making her wait."

Mike nodded. "Sure thing."

"Thanks." Josh patted him on the arm and then jogged towards the glowing tail lights of Agent Sterling's blue sedan.

Twenty minutes later, Josh and the federal agents were rolling around winding turns that passed larger and larger farms south of St. Claire. Wherever Perry was taking them was well hidden. Josh grabbed the arm rest of the door when the back of the car started to fishtail as the road curved.

"Oops." Perry turned the wheel trying to regain control.

Josh clenched his teeth and glared at the back of their heads. "You should've accepted my offer to drive."

Perry glanced into the rearview mirror. "I'm doing better than this guy." He smacked Agent Sterling's arm. "But, it's hard for anyone. Driving in snow like this."

Josh nudged the back of his seat. "It's harder for some people maybe."

"We're getting close, anyway." Agent Sterling looked down at the map displaying on his smart phone.

That reminded Josh of a question he'd thought of earlier but never asked. "Why do you have a safe house so close to St. Claire anyway?" Why did his home town hold so much interest from both criminals and cops?

Perry ducked his head and brought his face closer to the windshield like he was trying harder to see through the snow. "It's a recent purchase. When I found out who Nikki's parents were during our search for her ex, I got the bosses to divert some funds to purchase an old farmhouse here. Made a pitch that even if it never needed to be used in connection to Rob Appleton or his sister, we could use it for others being put in WITSEC. An area like this is a good place to stash someone temporarily if they're a cooperative witness who won't go into town and be pointed out by the locals." He flicked on his left turn signal. "Here we go."

The sedan slowed and turned onto a gravel driveway in front of a farmhouse. The chipping paint made it look more gray than white.

Perry came to a stop along the side of the house and the sound of the engine died only to be replaced by the unmistakable bang of a gunshot. Josh's head jerked in the direction of the blast, sending a sharp stab of pain down his spine. It had come from inside the house. Josh pushed the release of his seat belt, noticing Perry and Agent Sterling scrambling to do the same.

Agent Sterling glanced over his shoulder at Josh. "You stay here."

"Yeah, sure." Josh pulled the door handle and pushed his way out of the car, grabbing his service weapon from his side as he sprinted towards the front door of the house. Was it the Snitch? Had he come for Vaughn?

Josh swung open a ratted screen door and turned the door handle but it didn't budge. "It's locked." He heard the other men's footsteps coming up the stairs behind him.

Josh took two steps back and sucked in a breath before kicking just above the rusted handle. Wood splinters exploded into the air as the door flung open. Josh raised his gun and charged in only to stop after no more than a few steps inside.

He stood in a bare living room area. Vaughn was at his feet, red blood spreading across the chest of his blue prison jump suit. Quickly glancing around the room, he spotted Abigail also on the floor. Her cheek was busted open, and the sleeve of her blazer was torn with blood dripping down her arms. She was gagging, a wild expression on her face and the gun she had clearly just fired still in her hands.

She looked at Josh, and then her eyes darted to her superior officer. "P-Perry... Sir, it happened so fast. He had a weapon." She nodded to a piece of glass on the floor beside Vaughn. One end had been thickly wrapped in tape to create a makeshift handle. "He must have had it when we left the prison. Everything seemed fine, and then he got the jump on me. I had no choice. He was going to kill me—" Her words turned into sobs.

Josh crouched to his knees, still eyeing her gun. He lowered a hand feeling the side of Vaughn's neck. "He's dead."

***

Something poked Nikki's back, prickling down her spine. Even though her eyes were heavy with sleep, she forced them open. Everything was blurry in the dark, but she smelled something like grass and animals. Blinking, she made herself focus. She was lying down and thick, rough blankets were wrapped around her and her coat topped them like a much shorter covering. She placed her hands beneath her and pushed, feeling the same prickling sensation on her palms as she sat up. She'd been laying on a pile of hay. *Where am I?*

Moonlight shone through the gaps between the wood planks that made up the walls around her. Cold air swirled. Was she in a barn? She rolled onto her hands and knees and crawled forward but a hand grabbed her arm.

"Be careful. A few more inches and you'll fall off the side."

Nikki turned her head to see Rob holding her back and remembered the wreck, riding in the car with him, and then passing out from exhaustion. But was it exhaustion? It had come on so fast. Her head pounded. Maybe she'd hit her head harder than she remembered? Her muscles felt stiff, and her dried jeans rubbed against the stinging burns on her shins. She looked back in the direction she'd been going, squinting into the darkness. She slid her hand forward. The wood felt scratchy against her skin and then it stopped. She peered over the edge and saw empty horse stalls. They were in a hayloft.

A soft light flickered on. Her brother held out a small lantern that illuminated the area. Why did he bring her to a barn? *And how did I get up here?* "Where are we?"

He gave a half smile. "We'll only be here for tonight. There are a lot of police cars out looking for you, and eventually, they are going to track down the car I was driving. I ditched it in the woods after I got you settled up here."

Nikki peered through a gap in the wall and caught sight of a familiar farmhouse. "I know where we are. The couple that lives on this farm is very nice. We could probably just ask them if we could stay the night inside and not out in the cold." Shivering, she pulled the blankets up under her chin.

"No." Rob's voice was short and clipped. "I'm not trusting anyone in this place. I'll get another car in the morning, and we'll make a break for it."

Nikki sat back on her heels. Make a break for it? Why would she want to make a break for anything? "What do you mean by getting a car? Do you mean steal one?" Her stomach churned. Her brother was a criminal. How else could he have gotten the car he drove away from the accident or these blankets? What else has he stolen?

Rob let out a long breath. "Yes, I mean steal one. We're in danger. A lot more danger than whoever's car we'd be stealing is in."

Nikki grabbed the blankets and pulled them back around her. "I don't understand. Where are we even going? What about Josh? I need to know that he is okay. I'm supposed to marry him. Not to mention, he wouldn't want me to steal a car." She couldn't just fall into the same class as her parents.

Rob clenched his jaw and pointed a finger in her face. "Trust me. He's done a lot worse. You should be scared of a guy like that. A guy who's working with the Snitch."

She shook her head. If only she could look back on every moment since last night. She'd avoided Josh and had been wrapped up in her fear. Maybe if she had studied him she would have some kind of assurance as to his character now. "Like what? I-I just don't see that. Josh is a good, Godly man."

Rob put a hand on her shoulder. "He's a liar."

Nikki chewed her lip. "It can't all be a lie though. I felt it. Not just loving Josh, but I felt peace and grace." Tears welled in her eyes. "I found forgiveness. God loves me. God cares about what happens to me. Josh showed me that." Peace seeped into her heart as she said the words out loud.

Rob tilted his head to the side. "Man, what did he do to you? It's like he brainwashed you. No one is looking out for you but *me*." Her brother rubbed his neck with a hand. "He was just manipulating you. Life doesn't work like that. There isn't some all-powerful being who is just going to make everything better. No one is going to fight for you, Nikki. You have to fight for yourself. It's just you and me. Josh just wanted to make you loyal to him so you would do *exactly this*. So, you would doubt the truth. The *real* truth."

No. He had to be wrong. Sure it had been hard for her to believe at first. Back then, she couldn't accept that forgiveness and peace were just a prayer away. In her mind, nothing could be that easy. But Rob was her brother. If she couldn't convince him she was right, could she just abandon him? He'd been alone all his life, too. Maybe she should give him the benefit of the doubt.

Abigail's description of him popped into her mind. The agent had made him out to be a genius. Nikki never saw herself as dumb or gullible but she'd never hacked into computers before either.

Was it really out of the realm of possibility that her brother was right? Maybe she was right to doubt. Maybe it wasn't easy. Maybe there was nothing bigger to believe in. Maybe she was stuck with every bad decision she'd ever made. Maybe she was completely and totally alone. But it all just felt so real. "I-I don't know, Rob. I don't feel right about running. We should go to the sheriff's station and ask them for help."

His eyes narrowed, and after a moment, he sighed. "Listen, let's just take the rest of the night. You need time to process what I've told you and rest. Of course, it seems unbelievable to you. Just think about what I've said for a while and get some more sleep. And then in the morning, if you still think the deputy can be trusted, I'll take you back to him."

A wave of dizziness washed over her at the memory of how close they'd come to dying in the accident. If only she could just call Josh and make sure he was okay and let him know she was safe. She pictured her phone in the front pocket of her purse. It had been on the floor by her feet when they were in the patrol car and was no doubt still there.

But what if Rob was right and Josh only wanted to keep tabs on her for the Snitch? Her head pounded so she laid back down, sinking deeper into the nest of blankets. Better to get sleep and recover first.

"Fine. We can stay here for tonight. And I'll make my decision in the morning."

Rob nodded and turned off the lantern. "Sounds like a deal. I'm beat anyway. I'm ready to snooze."

Nikki pulled the blankets and her coat up to her neck and leaned back against the prickly straw pile. She closed her eyes and prayed, hoping her words would be heard. *God, please be there. Please be real. Show me the truth.*

CHAPTER 14

THIS WAS NOT THE FIRST time Josh had been to Nadine General Hospital since his wife, Heather, had died, but he still felt her presence as he trailed Perry down the hall to Abigail's room. Just over there was the room where he'd held her hand and said goodbye.

Since then, the transformation in his heart from overwhelming grief to a renewed sense of purpose was a true miracle and a reminder that, with God, all things were possible. Nikki had been taken from him before, and he'd found her. He could do it again, but he needed the Lord's help.

Vaughn was dead and gone, along with the answers to any of Josh's lingering questions. They needed to wrap things up here and get back to the sheriff's station so they could look for leads.

"This is her." Perry motioned to an open door.

Josh followed the marshal into the hospital room.

Abigail sat on the edge of a hospital bed, batting away the hand of a nurse. "I'm fine. I don't need to be here."

The nurse huffed and stepped back in surrender before turning to Perry and Josh. "She's all yours, gentlemen."

Good. They could be on their way. "Are you saying she is cleared to leave?"

The nurse grunted. "We replaced the bandages she'd had on her head and some bruises are starting. Physically, she'll be fine. But the doctor wanted her to stay and see a trauma counselor. We have one but she's refusing. It's standard procedure after an assault. She'll just talk to her for a little while to make sure she has resources in case she starts to feel any symptoms of PTSD."

Perry stepped past him up to Abigail's bedside. "Then I think we should stay until you talk to this counselor."

Abigail jumped down from the bed, shaking her head. "No way. I'm fine. We need to go. We need to find Nikki and Rob."

Perry sat down on the edge of the mattress. "You just killed a man. And only a day after being assaulted while on duty."

Abigail's eyes went wide. "It was self-defense."

"I know that." Perry patted her arm. "But it's protocol that the incident be investigated and reviewed, and it's not going to look good if the record shows that you ignored hospital recommendations. You're staying right here for now."

"But—"

Perry held up a hand. "But nothing. That's an order. The deputy and I will go down to the cafeteria while you see the counselor and then we'll be back to take your statement."

Abigail plopped back onto the mattress. "Fine. But then I want back on the case. I'm not sitting this one out."

Perry raised an eyebrow. "We'll talk about that after they officially release you." He then tilted his head towards the door. "Let's go."

Once they were back in the hall, Josh followed Perry to the bank of elevators. "Do you really think that was a good idea? We don't have time to be hanging around here. Nikki could be anywhere."

Perry smacked the call button. "Do you have any clue where she is?"

"No." But he wasn't going to find any waiting around the hospital until morning.

The smudged, silver doors opened, and Perry stepped inside. "Then, we're going to work this case like any other."

Josh followed him. "So, what do you suggest we do?"

Perry leaned back against the wood paneled walls. "I put in a call to the home office. They're sending all Rob's files over to the sheriff's office. Luke called his office as well to get his stuff on our AWOL cop and the Snitch files. Like you suggested, maybe we'll find something in them."

Thank You, Lord. It was about time he had some information to dig through. It was going to be a long night. So, if he had to be at the hospital for awhile, he might as well down some coffee and recharge. The elevator came to a stop, and the door opened, revealing Agent Sterling yelling into his phone. Red faced, he pointed at the receiver like the person on the other end of the call could see him. Then he spotted them. "Just do it." And ended the call.

What now? They didn't need any more bad news. "What was that about?"

The agent waved him off. "Nothing. Just the office giving me trouble about releasing some of the files. It's fine though. I've got agents on route to assist, too." Agent Sterling looked past Josh and Perry and into the elevator they'd just exited. "Where's Abigail?"

"She's going to be here awhile, yet." Perry craned his neck down the hall like he was looking for a sign to point them in the right direction. "Then we'll take her somewhere to rest for the night."

"St. Claire Country Inn is the only place to stay in town but they are never really booked up so you should have no problem getting her a room." Josh started down the hall, motioning the others to follow.

Perry snorted. "Well, they're gonna be booked up when I'm done calling in the cavalry from the Pittsburgh office. I'm tired of being reactive. We need new information and we need it soon."

Josh was tired of it too. It was time to get on the offensive. "The cafeteria is this way. I suggest we get some coffee and see what—if anything—they have left to eat. I have a feeling it's going to be a long night."

***

How had she fallen asleep so easily earlier but was now wide awake? Sleep would be such an escape from the turmoil in her soul. What was she going to do come morning? Trust her brother and run away with him to who knew where or go back to Josh and potentially risk being killed?

No matter how hard she tried, she just couldn't picture Josh doing anything to hurt her. Her brother had given her nothing specific just his insistence that Josh was using her. The morning they'd discovered that her shop had been broken into and vandalized, she'd been so devastated. She'd wanted comfort, so she'd let herself feel the attraction to Josh that she'd been fighting since she'd first moved to St. Claire. Her fingers tingled as she remembered the feel of her hands on his chest. If only these blankets could be replaced with Josh's warmth that day when she slid up onto her toes, reaching for his lips. But he'd backed away, scared of taking advantage of her vulnerable state. If his relationship with her was just a cover for some nefarious purpose, why wouldn't he have made a move earlier or at least accepted her advances?

She'd raged at being rejected after putting herself out there. If he was just trying to get in her good graces, why would he have risked making her so mad? She flipped onto her back, listening to Rob's deep breathing as she stared up at the vaulted ceiling of the barn. Twinkling stars were visible through the cracks. It seemed that for a moment the snow had let up. If only God would give her a sign. If only He would write 'Josh is good' or 'Josh is bad' across the sky, or send her some other kind of message. Then she would know for certain that her faith in Josh and her faith in God had not been misplaced.

She shut out her thoughts letting in the silent night. Waiting, she listened for a miracle. She waited for a sign. Tears filled her eyes when the world stayed quiet. Was no sign a sign in itself? Was she truly alone in the world? Did she not get a sign because no one was there to give it? If only she could get a glimpse of God. If only she could see Him.

See. The word seemed stuck in her mind. It reminded her of something. A verse. A verse she'd read many times since she found the courage to believe.

Faith is the substance of things hoped for, the evidence of things not seen.

Of things not seen. Something in those words made an impression in her heart. Nikki didn't want to believe in something just because she saw it with her eyes. She wanted to believe because of what she knew in her heart. Faith was a risk. A risk of disappointment. But if she went through life doubting everything and everyone around her, that would be no kind of life at all.

Josh had faith in her even when he had no evidence to prove her innocence. How could she not do the same for him? Rob would have to believe in her. He'd have to believe that what she knew in her heart was true. That the God who put those stars above them saw the best in people and she would too. Peace filled her. This was the right decision.

Nikki would give Rob the night. But in the morning, she was going home.

CHAPTER 15

IT WAS ALMOST DAWN BEFORE Josh and the agents finally got Abigail to the Inn to rest and made their way to the sheriff's station. Josh felt sticky from the previous day. His uniform was still dirty from the car wreck, and his muscles ached. Once he got the others set up in the conference room, he would run down to the locker room to grab a shower and a change of clothes from his locker.

He wondered if Nikki felt the same fatigue wherever she was and hoped she didn't. *Lord, keep her safe until I find her.*

Sheena Haggarty waved to Josh from behind her desk as he pushed open the glass door to the sheriff's station. Josh motioned to the agents who were following behind. "Sheena, this is Marshal Cole and FBI Special Agent Sterling. They're with me."

The petite part-administrative-assistant part-dispatcher part-whatever-the-department-needed squinted at the suited men and then ran her eyes down Josh's dirt and blood-stained uniform. "You look like crap, Josh."

"Thanks." Josh snorted. Sheena could always be counted to speak the truth. "Is there anyone in the conference room?"

Sheena opened her mouth to answer when her desk phone began to ring, and she held up a finger telling him to wait. "Nadine County Sheriff's department." She tilted her head and raised her shoulder to pin the phone in the crook of her neck, freeing her hand to grab a pen and start scribbling on a note pad. Josh was about to turn and go look for himself when he heard the paper tear. She waved the paper at him. "Mr. Turner, I am sure Mrs. Turner did not poison you. Just like she didn't poison you last week. But I can send out some EMTs to take you to the hospital, all right?"

Josh bit back a smile took the paper. That colorful old couple was the stuff of St. Claire legend. He summarized the message for his companions. "She said some marshals brought in the files you wanted, Perry, and the FBI faxed us files on the Snitch like Agent Sterling requested. They're waiting for us in the briefing room."

Agent Sterling nodded to Sheena and grinned. "Poison, huh? Is it always this exciting in Hicksville?"

Here we go again. The agent was nothing if not consistent in his prejudice against small towns. Josh waved him off. "That's just old man Turner. He calls in a couple times a month to say his wife, Alice, is trying to kill him. He's er... eccentric."

Perry chuckled. "Well, if she didn't have a reason to kill him before, she sure does now."

Josh smiled as he pictured one of the kindest smiles he'd grown up seeing every Sunday at church. "Alice Turner is a dear. Come on. The briefing room is this way." Josh pointed to a narrow beige hallway as Sheena's phone slammed down.

"Josh, wait."

He paused. The two other men looked at him expectantly. "You guys go on ahead. It's the room at the end of the hall."

As soon as the agents started on their way, Josh turned back to Sheena. "What's up?"

She twisted a strand of her tightly curled brown hair. "Your sister is in the briefing room, too."

Lizzy? What was she doing here?

"She knew that Nikki was missing when she got here." Sheena tapped her nails on the desk. "I'm thinking—"

Josh cut in, already suspecting the truth. "Koby called her, I bet."

Sheena shrugged. "That'd be my guess. He's been in and out here, too. Might be back there now."

His big city lawyer sister and his best friend had been dating on and off all his teenage years until something terrible split them up for good. But no matter how much distance Lizzy put between them, they never could seem to be completely rid of each other. "Then I guess we'll have to see how long it takes for the yelling to start."

Sheena laughed. "We've already started a betting pool."

"Thanks for giving me the heads up." Josh took a step.

"That's not all," Sheena said. "You also missed Anna Duncan."

Josh furrowed his brow in confusion, and then it came to him. "Right. She wanted to talk to me. She said she had information about a relation of Nikki's. I completely forgot."

Sheena laid a hand on her phone. "Want me to see if she can come back?"

He'd hate to wake her but what if the information she had led them Nikki? "Yeah, you better. She may even be up and prepping right now so if you can't get her on her cell, call Poppy's. Tell her to get over here as fast as she can."

"Will do."

Josh nodded his thanks and then jogged down the hall to the briefing room. He half expected to walk in on his sister and Koby arguing, but Koby wasn't there at all. Instead, Lizzy sat at one of the tables, gently swiveling from one side to the other on a desk chair as she listened to Agent Sterling and Perry fight over the file boxes. She glanced at him through the gap between the agents' shoulders and smiled, but he caught a bit of sadness in her eyes.

"Hey, Joshie. We're going to find her. I know it." She jumped up from her seat and rushed to him, her arms open wide for a hug.

Josh matched the gesture and pulled her close, his arms crossing over her long strawberry blonde hair. "You didn't need to come down here." But inside, he was glad she did.

She took a step back and slapped his chest. "Of course, I did. And why didn't you call me and tell me all this was going on?" She motioned to the cut on his forehead then looked down his uniform, her face twisted in disgust.

Josh let his eyes drop to his shoes to avoid his sister's accusing stare. "I don't know. It all just happened so fast and there was nothing you could do."

Lizzy rolled her eyes. "Joshie, people *always* need their lawyer."

"You can be my lawyer anytime, girl." Agent Sterling gave his sister a wink.

Lizzy spun around. "I've got a feeling you are beyond help."

Josh knew he wouldn't have to scare the agent off. Lizzy was a firecracker and that guy had no clue who he was dealing with. "Well, I'm glad you're here now, sis. And since I'm guessing he was the one that told you what was going on, where's Koby?" His best friend wasn't in law enforcement but it would feel nice having another person hanging around that he could count on.

"I figured y'all would be hungry when you eventually got back so I sent him to get some food when Sheena gave us an ETA on your return. I was just in here staring at the wall when your federal friends came in." She motioned to Perry and Agent Sterling.

Perry raised the lid of a file box that was sitting on the table and fingered through the folders inside. "I got a feeling you did more than stare at the wall."

Lizzy spun around to face him. "Marshal Cole, I can't believe you would accuse me of looking at official government documents without authorization."

Perry threw back his head with a snort. "That wasn't exactly a denial."

Lizzy shrugged. "Why don't we just get to work—"

The briefing room door swung open.

Josh expected to see his best friend with arms full of food, but instead he saw Laney, the deputy sheriff, her face hardened with a serious look.

Josh rushed over to her. "Did one of the patrol cars find her? Is she hurt?"

"Oh. I'm sorry, no." Laney wiped a hand over her mouth like she was embarrassed. "I just came to say that the federal crime scene people you had sent down, Agent Sterling, are finished with the scene so they are taping up the house and closing it for now."

Josh let out a breath. Why would he care about that? They might be FBI, but he'd walked the scene personally. Chances were they'd find nothing. "Okay. Thanks for letting us know."

Laney adjusted the tight ponytail of graying hair on her head. "We'll keep looking for her, Josh. I've got everyone out there. Even the sheriff has been out patrolling since the minute we heard she was taken. We'll find a trail somewhere."

A warmth spread over Josh's chest as he thought about his boss, Sheriff Gary Thompson. Knowing a man as diligent and fearless as Gary was out there looking for his fiancée, brought him comfort. The old man *never* gave up. "Thanks, Laney. We're going to be in here going over files in case you hear anything I need to know."

Laney nodded and left them to it.

Lizzy joined Agent Sterling beside one of the tables and looked over his shoulder at the faxes he was sorting through. "So where do we start?"

Josh rubbed the back of his neck. He wasn't sure where they should start. How long would it take to find what they needed in this endless stack of paper? And that assumed they found something at all.

Josh moved up beside his sister and watched Agent Sterling spread papers out onto the table. Something caught Josh's attention, and he reached out a hand, letting his fingertip stop on a black and white photo in the middle of the table. "Why do you have a picture of Rob Appleton in the FBI files? He was in the marshal's custody, so the FBI wouldn't have been keeping tabs on him."

Agent Sterling furrowed his brow. "What are you talking about?"

Josh tapped the photo on the table, the thuds of his fingers emphasizing his point. "Why do you have this picture of Nikki's brother. This is the guy that came to her house last night. He's the one who has her now."

"Deputy." Agent Sterling snatched the picture off the table and poked his finger at the figure in it. "*That* is not Nikki's brother."

***

Nikki wasn't sure if it was her hunger or the sun that woke her up, but when she finally came to, her stomach was growling, and she had to blink away the rays of sun low on the horizon that were streaming through the boards of the barn.

"I've got some food." Her brother's voice was soft.

Nikki sat up, wincing as her muscles punished her for moving. Yawning, she rubbed the sleep out of her eyes before she spotted the granola bar in Rob's outstretched hand. Compelled by her gut, she snatched it and tore into the wrapper, ravenously gobbling the bar down.

A bottle of water was handed to her next. "Thanks." She sat it beside her while she chewed and started picking pieces of hay out of her scarf bundled up on the loose straw next to her. "I'm pretty sure I won't, but I'd really like to forget about sleeping in a barn."

Rob chuckled. "Don't worry. We're leaving. I've been keeping an eye on the house. Seems quiet. Like everyone is still asleep. There's an old truck in a garage by the house. I should be able to get it started. Then, I have a plan of where to go next."

Nikki swallowed. "About that... I-I was thinking last night as I went to sleep and... praying and, well, I've come to a decision."

Rob let out a long breath. "And?"

Was this the right decision? Rob was her brother. Her only family. No, she had made her decision and she felt peace. "I know you have doubts about Josh, and I believe you if you say someone in the marshals service is working for the Snitch. But I just don't believe Josh is capable of what you are saying. I know it in my heart. I mean, you could be wrong about him, right?"

Rob narrowed his gaze. "I'm not wrong. Did you forget all I told you last night? Do you really think him being in your life is a coincidence?"

Nikki's chest tightened. *Lord, help him understand.* Was he really going to ask her to choose? Her brother or her fiancé? What would she do? "I admit that some of what you said sounded suspicious, but Josh believed in me when no one else did. I have to do the same for him. I have to have faith."

"Faith." His face twisted in disgust. "You're living in a fantasy."

Nikki straightened her spine, holding her head high. "Look, I understand if you can't go back with me. If you can't take that risk. But I have to go back. I have to see what Josh has to say about your vague accusations that he's a liar and if I feel he's not the man I think he is, there are other people I can turn to for help. There may be bad guys in the Marshals or even in the FBI, but Gary, the sheriff, and the deputy sheriff, Laney. I trust them. They'll keep me safe."

Rob raised an eyebrow. "Some people aren't who you think they are."

Nikki shrugged. "And some people are."

"Well, it seems like your mind's made up. Let me just get my things and then we'll head back."

"Thank you."

Her brother stood and crossed over to his bag. As he leaned over, the back of his black T-shirt rode up revealing smooth skin across the gap.

Nikki froze. Her lungs seemed about to burst as if she'd forgotten how to breathe, and her heart forgot how to beat. Perry's voice echoed through her memory.

Your brother—he was only seven at the time—freed himself before the paramedics made it to the scene. It was a miracle he survived. He had broken bones and a burn down his back that would scar him for the rest of his life...

There was no scar on this man's back. No marks she saw evidence of at all. That could only mean one thing: this man was not Rob Appleton. But for some reason, he wanted her to believe he was her brother. Was he working for the Snitch? Trying to use her to lure her real brother out of hiding? Fear urged her to scream, and her aching body was desperate to obey. She started to shiver and clenched her fists in her lap. Stay calm. Pretend everything was fine.

She recalled bits of the ride away from the accident. After she drank the water he'd given her, she'd felt exhausted and passed out within seconds. What if that hadn't been her adrenaline levels dropping? What if he had drugged her so she wouldn't have kept trying to go back for Josh?

Rob, or rather pseudo-Rob, was still digging through the bag, and she was certain she wasn't going to like whatever he pulled out of it. She had to act. What were her options?

Run maybe? Escape had to be the first priority, right? What would Josh do? Her instinct was to flee. She pictured what she'd seen of the outside through the planks and what she remember about the Turner's land. There was a thick forest in the distance that she could hide in, but she would have to clear an open field to reach it and if this imposter was going to pull out a gun, she'd never make it. It wasn't like she was faster than a bullet.

Somehow, she needed to delay him. A head-start just might get her to the tree line. Nikki laid her palms on the ground beside her thighs, careful not to crush the patches of hay around her. Not taking her eyes off her captor, she spun her feet behind her, curling her toes onto the wood. Then not daring to breathe, she leaned back on her heels and pushed herself to her feet.

She could act like she was getting ready and gather her coat and scarf and shake off the hay like she didn't want to track it into the Turner's truck. Would he buy it if she said she was going to climb down the ladder and stretch out her legs on the barn floor? Then, she'd at least be on the ground when she made a break for it.

The imposter's arm went still in the bag, like his hand had touched what he was looking for. He lifted out a black, electronic device that Nikki recognized from a similar one that hung the utility belt Josh wore with his uniform. A taser. Not a pistol but still scary. This could work. Tasers could only go a certain distance, and if she moved in a serpentine pattern, like Josh had told her to do if she were ever fleeing for her life, she might be able to get away.

142

Nikki took a backward step in the direction of the wooden ladder but when she took a second step, the plank creaked under the ball of her foot.

The imposter spun to face her. Forget about her coat. Forget the plan. Forget stealth. There was nothing else to do but run. Nikki lunged for the ladder but a hand wrapped around her bicep and jerked her back. Something Josh had once told her flashed through Nikki's mind. *If they're bigger than you, use their strength against them.* Nikki didn't fight the stranger but let him swing her around so that his force would be added to her own. She raised an arm as he spun her around, and just as she was about to crash into his chest, she jammed the heel of her hand up into his nose.

Something cracked against her palm, and the imposter cried out in pain. His hands sprang to his face, and her arm fell free. She looked in the direction of a clattering sound and saw the taser in the hay. Nikki scooped it up and scrambled to the ladder.

The rough wood splintered into her skin as she slid down the rungs, sprawling onto the dirt floor of the barn. Jumping to her feet, she took off in a sprint, snow flying up with every step once she'd exited the barn. Adrenaline coursed through her but fear still nipped at her heels urging her to move faster and faster. The trees were close now, but she felt no peace. The imposter was sure to chase after her. True, she'd claimed a small victory and even a weapon, but this fight was nowhere near the end. Soon he'd steal the truck and have a clear path to follow in the snow. Once she reached the trees, she'd have to disguise her trail and avoid the roads until she found some help.

The sun disappeared as she crossed the tree line, and a stone-cold chill passed through her. Her skin seemed to be burning in the cold. Her bare arms felt raw. If only she'd had time to grab her coat, she might be okay but—exposed like this—she wouldn't last long. She was running out of time. If her pursuer didn't get her, the elements would.

CHAPTER 16

LIZZY RAN A HAND THROUGH her hair and groaned. "If that man is not Rob Appleton, who is he?"

Josh sank down in one of the worn desk chairs around the conference room table. How had this happened? Why hadn't he thought to confirm that the man who had been sitting across the table from him at Nikki's house was who he said he was? Could he be working for the Snitch? And if so, what was he doing to Nikki right now?

Perry knocked his head with the heel of his hand, his face grim. "His name is Kent Marcus. He's the Pittsburgh police officer who went AWOL after Vaughn was arrested."

Josh flashed back to Apple's when Perry had told them the danger wasn't over and tossed a stack of photographs onto the table "He was the cop who was following her? The one who had all those pictures of her?"

Perry nodded. "We're not sure why he took off. Maybe he thought Vaughn would tip us off to whatever he was doing?"

Lizzy moved up beside him and squeezed his shoulder. "What does he want her for?"

Agent Sterling lifted the page with the grainy photo of Kent. "I think we have to assume that he's working for the Snitch."

He'd had pictures of her family. He knew who her parents were. That was the only explanation.

"Or maybe he is the Snitch."

Josh swiveled to find Koby in the doorway, hands full of take-out bags. He hadn't even heard him open the door. Josh got to his feet. "Hey, man."

Kobby shifted the bags to one arm and hit Josh on the shoulder. "We're going to find her, brother. I know it."

"Thanks." Josh could barely muster a smile. He thought he'd been diligent. He'd thought he could protect her but when it came down to it, Josh really couldn't save anyone. Only God was in control.

Lizzy stepped up beside them to take the bags, then began pulling out cartons and setting them on the table.

"He's too young to be him." Josh turned and saw Agent Sterling eyeing his sister before jerking his head towards Koby. "How do you even know that name? Have we forgotten there's a criminal in this town somewhere?" He smacked the side of a chair and sent it spinning. "Can any hillbilly that walks into this building look through official government files like it's nothing?"

Koby glared at the agent. "Well, someone needed take a closer look at the situation because it seems you guys can't even keep names and faces straight."

Josh held up his hands. Agent Sterling was right that they didn't need all their details spread out and about, but he didn't need to be a jerk about it. "Everybody just calm down. The more eyes on this the better." His best friend wasn't a rash man but he'd respond if provoked. And they didn't need that right now.

"Back to the main question, Koby, he's right." Josh motioned to Perry. "According to Perry, this Snitch guy was in business before Nikki and her brother were even born. We've got to be looking for someone close to fifty at least."

"Fine." Koby grabbed a carton and a plastic fork off the table and plopped into the open chair closest to where his sister was doling out the food.

Lizzy let out a long breath as she looked down into an open carton. "Chinese food? Really. You couldn't have gone to Bieler's."

Koby shoved a fork full of noodles in his mouth. "I had a hankering."

"Whatever." She rolled her eyes as she took the seat next to him. I hate that the Snitch may be connected to someone I know."

Josh's stomach growled. He didn't want to listen to it. He'd rather be out there finding Nikki, but since he had no clue where to start looking, he might as well refuel while he had the chance. Josh grabbed an egg roll off the table and slumped down in his chair. "This guy may be too young, but the law enforcement angle makes a lot of sense."

Perry crossed his arms over his chest, ignoring the food on the table. "You think the Snitch is a cop?"

Josh swallowed. "It would kind of make sense, wouldn't it? If he is, he can track the movements of the criminals *and* the cops. And let's not forget that Rob, the *real* Rob, ditched his marshal protection. Why would he do that if one of them didn't scare him?"

Perry scrunched up his face. "We don't know that. I'm not ready to just jump on the notion that someone in my organization is dirty. That said, we've already been operating under a misconception. We have no clue where Rob really is. The Snitch could already have him for all we know. He could've stolen him from WITSEC in the first place, and we just assumed he ran off."

Josh's jaw grew sore as chewed another bite. Had the accident knocked something loose? He dropped the rest of the egg roll on the table. Maybe Sheena would have some over the counter pain pills. "I don't think so. If they had him, they would have gotten what they wanted, killed him, and been on their way."

"Unless they do have him and he won't talk." Agent Sterling picked through his carton, looking at it like it had gone bad. "They may want to use her to get it out of him. He may not care what happens to himself but if they get her in front of him, he'll probably say anything to keep her from getting hurt."

Josh watched his sister hold herself tight. There was a tortured look in her eyes like she was imagining what these guys would do to Nikki to get her brother to talk. Josh saw Koby watching too. Koby raised a hand like was going to touch her shoulder. Like he was going to comfort her but after a second of hesitation, he let his arm fall back to his side.

Josh felt a tinge of sadness for his friend. There was a time when Lizzy would've welcomed Koby's embrace but there was so much history between them now. But it was easy to see they could never forget what they'd had. Josh bet that the impulse to reach for each other when things got rough would always be there.

If Agent Sterling wanted to make a connection with Lizzy, he'd have to fight his way through pretty deep roots.

"Maybe." Josh pulled himself back to the topic at hand. "If that's true, it means she's still alive."

"Until they get what they want." Agent Sterling gestured with his fork like he was a teacher pointing at a blackboard.

Perry tapped the tabletop. "Then we have no time to lose."

Josh reached out a hand towards the FBI agent. "Can I see the file you have on Kent? Maybe it'll tell us a place he'd take her."

"I feel like they're still in town," Koby mumbled, his mouth half full of food.

Agent Sterling squinted at him. "Why?"

Koby swallowed. "Because this is where Rob would go. The real Rob. If he left because he was scared of a marshal, he'd want to make sure his only family member was safe, too. He would've come for her. Maybe we've just gotten in his way by guarding her too close. That's what I would do."

If Lizzy was in danger, Josh would come for her too.

Agent Sterling sneered. "Well, if the mechanic says so."

"Okay." Perry knocked a fist on the table. "That's enough. Let's just relax. We have to start somewhere."

"Koby's right." Josh was over the bickering. It was time to get to work. "Perry, why don't you and Agent Sterling go through the Kent and Snitch files and list any known locations connected with them. Koby and I will list any local locations we know of where someone might try to hide out."

Agent Sterling bit his bottom lip and then replied. "Fine. My men are almost here. We'll turn this place upside down looking."

Josh pushed his feet against the floor, sending his chair rolling back as he stood. "I'll go get us all some coffee from the break room. I'm sure we're going to need it."

Josh swung open the briefing room door and stepped out into the hall, smacking right into Sheena. "Whoops." She yelped as she fell to the side.

Josh grabbed her arm, pulling her upright. Had she been out here eavesdropping? "I'm so sorry. I should've watched where I was going."

She waved him off. "I wasn't watching either. I was on my way to get coffee." She held up her mug. "I just got off the phone. Mr. Turner called again, and I realized I needed some caffeine. With everyone out for the search, who knows when I'll get out of here."

Josh chuckled and pointed down the hall. Why was he suspecting his friend all of sudden? Where was his faith? "I'm on my way there too. We'll go together." Poor Alice. *Lord, give her patience.*

A few seconds later, Josh scooped coffee grounds into a filter.

Sheena stirred cream into her mug with a black plastic stirrer. Being the gentleman, he'd let her take the last in the pot and was starting a new batch. "That old man is going to turn me paranoid too, if he keeps this up."

Josh smiled. "What's he's saying about Alice now? Is he still on the poison thing?"

Sheena tossed the stirrer into the trash can sitting beside the counter and puffed out a breath. "No, I was able to talk him out of that one. He's now saying Mrs. Turner has hired a hitman who is hiding in their barn, waiting to strike."

Hitman? Josh sat the bag of grounds onto the counter. "Why does he think that?"

"Says he found 'evidence' that the assassin was in there. Said he went out to feed the cows a bit ago and found a water bottle and food wrappers and—get this—blood."

Josh's breath caught. "Blood?"

Sheena took a sip and then continued. "It's probably red paint. I saw Alice at Apple's the other day and she told me they just added a new coat to the barn."

His heart raced. "Did he find anything else?"

Sheena narrowed her gaze. "Uh… yeah, actually. A women's coat and scarf. It's probably his wife's."

Josh grabbed her arms, feeling his racing pulse in his fingertips. "The scarf, what did it look like?"

Sheena flinched, pulling away from him. Coffee splashed out on to her wrist.

Josh grabbed a napkin and handed it to her, telling himself to calm down. He hadn't meant to scare her. "I'm sorry, but it may have to do with Nikki's disappearance."

Her eyes widened in realization. "Of course. Um… He said it was green."

***

Nikki's chest burned. *Help me, Lord. I can't last another second.* Had she ever run this far in her whole life? Her quivering muscles had demanded a rest but now every breath sounded like thunder. It was as if the snow blanketing the ground soaked up every sound not coming from her and silence was her only hope. There was no doubt in her mind that the man pretending to be her brother would have followed her. And given that she'd made her flight through snow, tracking her would be easy.

She was at least a head shorter than the imposter. It would only be a matter of time until he caught her. Her fingers clutched the bark of the tree. She'd crouched beside it when she knew she couldn't take another step. The voice in her head said to look around the trunk and see if he was following her, but fear kept her frozen. She didn't want to know. She didn't want to see. Sucking in another shaky breath, she swallowed it down, trying to hear anything besides the pounding of her own heart.

What was that? She gripped the taser tighter. It sounded like water. Like *running* water. A creek maybe? The snow might leave breadcrumbs for the imposter to follow but there were no footprints in water. Nikki let out her breath in a white, frozen cloud. A second wind from who knew where rushed over her and she jumped to her feet, sprinting towards the sound. She had to get to the creek and fast. It was her best chance.

Nikki's path took her down a sloping hill. About twenty steps into her flight, her foot slipped in the wet snow, and she fell, beginning to roll. Scared of the rocks that were certain to be under the layer of snow, she held her arms over her head and surrendered to gravity. When she finally hit the bottom of the valley, she heard a splash, and her hand seemed to fall into a nest of sewing needles as the taser fell free. Shaking the snow from her face, she opened her eyes and groaned. She was laying beside the creek, her right hand in the frigid cold, and there was no sign of the taser. It must have been lost downstream. With nothing to defend herself with now except distance, she really needed to get out of there.

The stream branched out to her right and left. Once the imposter discovered that her footprints ended at the water's edge, he would know that she had followed the creek, but he wouldn't know which direction. She had a fifty-fifty chance he would go the wrong way. She couldn't hope for any better odds.

Wait a minute. What was that on the other side of the water? Nikki squinted to see through the trees and then gasped from excitement.

It was a hunter's blind, resting high up on stilts. A ladder rested on the side at an opening cut out of the wood. Her odds on the creek might still end up at fifty-fifty, but maybe she could delay his decision. She rushed into the water, heading for the blind. Once through the water, she let her feet fall heavy in the snow so there was no chance the imposter would miss her prints. She made sure to walk straight to the ladder and then turned back being careful to only step in the prints she already made until she got back to the water.

Seeing unmistakable footprints, the imposter would have to check the blind but by then, she could be far down the creek and then, even if he did choose the same direction, she would at least have a good head-start. The instant her feet hit the water she started to her right and then, she heard the sound of snow being crushed under feet. He was coming. He'd caught up with her. Had her brilliant plan to mislead him just led to her capture?

Her eyes darted around. She needed something. Anything. Was there a weapon of some kind? Maybe a rock from the creek bed? Or a hiding place? Nikki noticed one of the many bushes along the bank was still green under the snow and then glanced back at the path she'd made. Maybe her plan wouldn't be all for naught. Nikki dove at the roots, shimmying under the long, thick branches until she'd made herself as small as she could underneath it. Then she held still so the branches wouldn't move and listened.

The imposter came along a moment later. The lower half of his face was pink and red with the blood from his nose smeared across his mouth like a violent smile. The palm Nikki had used to cause the damage tingled at the sight of it.

The imposter reached the water's edge. He glanced over both his shoulders and then crossed over and followed her steps to the blind. Now was her chance. He was on the ladder now. Climbing. The instant his foot pushed off the last rung, Nikki rolled from under the brush and onto her feet in the water.

The imposter disappeared into the blind, and Nikki started moving through the water, Crouching next to the bush-crowded bank, she moved on the balls of her feet. Had her plan worked? Was she going to get away?

She heard a snap and turned to her side. A dark blur and then he was on top of her. The icy water hit her like a slap when she went in, and her head went under. She screamed. Air bubbles from her mouth shot up to the surface. A hand wrapped around her hair and pulled her up. She sucked in a deep breath and then screamed.

Nikki squirmed and elbowed and crawled over the mud and pebble paste of the creek bed until she wrenched herself free. She tried to scurry away on hands and knees, but he caught her ankle.

"No!" Nikki flipped onto her back and kicked out her free foot, aiming for her attacker's already-injured nose.

The man bellowed in pain as her heel hit his face, and her ankle was free. Scrambling to her feet, Nikki ran, splashing up water with every step.

"I have a gun. Stop or I'll shoot you!"

Nikki stopped. Was he lying? She had only seen the taser earlier. Maybe there was no gun at all. Or maybe... there was. Nikki turned around, her hands and legs shaking from exhaustion and the cold.

His bag was slung over his shoulder and he pointed a silver pistol at her that wasn't a stun gun but an actual bullet-loaded weapon, pointed right at her.

"Who are you? Why are you doing this?"

She got no answer. Instead he reached into his back pocket and pulled out a cell phone. He shook the water off it and quickly inspected the screen like he was checking to see if the splashes of water had damaged it. After a few seconds, he tapped on the screen and held it up to his ear.

"I need to be picked up." He paused. "I know I'm not where I'm supposed to be. There was a complication, and I don't care if it's inconvenient for you." He glared at Nikki, but then his eyes went wide, and his brow crinkled. "You're close by? Why? What?" Her attacker glanced back at the trees in the direction they'd come.

Who was coming for him? Now she was going to really be outnumbered. She followed his gaze. She couldn't see anything but heard shouting. They were calling her name!

"Come on." He used the gun barrel to motion her out of the water. "Follow me."

Did he think she was an idiot? Nikki stood straighter. "No."

Her attacker snarled at her. "Do you *want* me to kill you?"

Nikki wouldn't back down. "Of course not. But I'm not going with you. You tried to use a taser on me first not a gun. It seems like you need me for something."

He glanced from her to the direction of the voices. He growled, then disappeared into the trees.

Nikki waited until she couldn't see him anymore so he wouldn't turn back and shoot her from the opposite tree line before letting out the heaving breath that she seemed to have been holding her whole life and screamed. "I'm here!"

CHAPTER 17

"SHE WAS HERE." JOSH CROUCHED over the drops of blood next to what Josh was certain was Nikki's crumpled coat and scarf in the Turner's hayloft.

Perry peered over his shoulder. "That blood ain't that old neither."

"There's more out here."

Josh turned at the sound of Agent Sterling's voice outside and then glanced up at the marshal. "Let's go."

They climbed down the ladder and Josh ran outside as Perry yelled to one of the other FBI agents to get some evidence bags and a camera up there for some pictures. Agent Sterling and Mike and Brandon Whittaker had formed a circle around something on the ground.

Josh blinked away a snowflake caught on his eye lashes and looked down at what they were guarding. It was a boot print with pinkish slush spread across the heel.

Agent Sterling motioned down to his shoes. "It's mine. The ground was white when I walked over here, but then this showed up when I took a step. The snow is covering the trail, but the blood leads out here."

Brandon crossed his arms over his chest. "She could've been injured when they left. He had to have had a car or something. But I don't see any recent tire tracks."

They could be out of town already then. Unless... "Maybe they didn't flee in a car."

Like he was reading his mind, the sheriff called, "We've got footprints."

Josh jogged towards the edge of the barnyard where Sheriff Gary Thompson and Laney stood motioning to two sets of indentations in the snow.

The falling snow was filling them in but Josh judged they were still recent. She was close. *Lord, help me find her.* "We need to follow the trail before this snow covers it completely." Josh started jogging alongside them. "They're heading into the tree line." He called over his shoulder and picked up the pace.

The footfalls behind him grew faster. Perry's voice broke the silence.

"Some of these prints overlap each other. I'd say that meant he was pushing her ahead of him but the strides are too long. That would indicate they were running."

Josh heart skipped a beat. "She must've escaped and made a run for it. Then he chased her."

Agent Sterling ran up beside him. "There are no return prints. So, he either caught her and left the area another way or—"

"Or he's still chasing her." Josh puffed out the words as he crossed the tree line. "We need to move faster." His eyes were adjusting to the dimmer light."Nikki!"

The forest remained silent except for his racing breaths and then—finally—one clear and perfect, "I'm here," broke the silence.

Her voice was the sweetest sound he'd ever heard. Leaping over snow covered roots bulging up out of the ground, Josh weaved through trees.

A second passed, and then he heard her again along with the sound of rushing water. Closer. "I'm here!"

He nearly choked when he saw her through the thick snow. She was making her way out of the creek below. She was soaked head to toe. That water had to be freezing. She was holding herself tightly and even from a distance he could see her limbs shaking with cold. How long had she been out here? In this cold, in that shape, frostbite or hypothermia could take hold in less than an hour. He needed to get her warm and probably to the hospital.

Josh started pulling off his coat as he closed in on her. She was trying to run to him but it was if the ground had shackled her feet. Her face twisted with determination, but she only seemed to get slower. She reached out to him. "H-He wasn't my brother."

Josh threw the coat around her shoulders like a cape and pulled her against his chest. "I know, baby."

Her whole body spasmed in his arms. She raised a shaking hand and pointed farther into the woods. "He r-ran off when we heard you coming. He's g-getting away."

"Let him. I just want you." Josh braced her against him with one arm and then reached down behind her knees with the other, scooping her up into his arms. "We need to get you out of the cold."

Josh turned back towards the Turner's property and started hurrying, holding Nikki tight. He paused when Perry and Agent Sterling caught up. "He went that way." Josh nodded back towards the creek. "You should be able to follow his tracks. I have to get her somewhere warm."

Perry motioned for Agent Sterling to pursue the scumbag and then turned back to Josh. "Want me to radio for an ambulance?"

Nikki's lips moved against his chest. "I don't want to go to the hospital." The words were muffled and soft. No good would come from arguing out here in the cold.

Josh shook his head and resumed his trek up the hill. "I'll call for one when we get back to the house." Her hand balled up the fabric of his shirt. "If we need one." At that, she seemed to relax against him.

He called over his shoulder. "Just find him, Perry."

***

Nikki couldn't see much as she huddled against her fiancé but what she did see was unsteady and fluid with movement as Josh charged through the trees. The Turner's farmhouse came into view, but it was blurry like a mirage. The image sharpened as they got close, and Nikki saw other law enforcement vehicles. She was safe. *Thank You, Lord.* Josh may have found her, but she knew in her heart that God had been the one to send him her way.

When Josh headed for the house instead of vehicles she sighed with relief. Rest was coming. Alice Turner appeared on the porch as they approached.

"Oh my word." Alice gasped as Josh's heavy boots boomed up the porch steps. "She's wet down to the bone. You'd better bring her inside." She held open the screen and motioned for Josh to go ahead of her. "George, put on some hot water for tea."

When Josh carried her over the threshold, the warmth from the house was like fire on her skin. Tensing from the pain, she focused on Josh's voice instead.

"We need to get her dry." He was panting.

Alice grabbed the edge of a blanket off the back of an arm chair and laid it over Nikki. "Don't." Nikki pushed weakly at her hand. "Your blanket will get all wet."

"Nonsense, dear." The older woman tucked it in tight. "Josh, bring her upstairs."

Josh followed their hostess to the dark-stained staircase.

The wool fibers of the afghan sent little needles across Nikki's cheeks as they climbed to the second floor. Faces from framed pictures watched her as they moved down a long hall. Every captured moment was filled with the members of a large family. Hot tears stung her frozen cheeks. She'd thought she finally had a family. Where was her real brother? And how did the imposter get those pictures?

Josh turned into a small bedroom that was made even smaller by a large sleigh bed.

"Set her down here." Alice patted the mattress. "I'll go find something warm for her to wear."

When he laid her down, she sat upright and Josh pulled his coat tighter around her shoulders and tucked the blanket under her chin as he kneeled in front of her. "You're going to be okay." He cupped her cheeks with his hands.

Nikki nodded, not wanting to try and talk through her still-chattering teeth.

Alice reappeared, a pile of clothes in her hands. "Emily left some things here before she went back to graduate school that I think will work perfectly."

Josh kissed Nikki's forehead and then got to his feet. "Thank you so much, Mrs. Turner."

"Don't you even mention it." She smiled before ushering him out of the room. "Now you wait out here while I help her get changed." Turning to Nikki, the older woman flashed her a sympathetic smile. "Let's get you warm and dry."

Nikki bit at her quivering lip and pushed Josh's coat off her shoulders. "I'm sorry I brought all this to your door. What if you or your family had been hurt or—"

Soft fingers pressed against her lips. "You shush about that. Nothing happened. God was watchin' out for all of us today." She laid the coat and afghan over the foot board and then wrapped an arm around Nikki's back and helped her stand. "Let's get you out of these clothes before you turn blue."

The changing process was like ripping off a bandage. It hurt but was for the best. Nikki didn't want to move but with some coaxing, Alice helped her get toweled off and changed. She even took the care to brush out her hair.

Never had an outfit been as comforting as the sweatshirt and leggings that replaced the frozen and dirty rags her clothes had become.

Alice pulled back the quilt once she was fully clothed. "You get under the covers, dear."

The last of the adrenaline seemed to flow out of her as her head hit the pillow.

There was a soft knock on the door. "Ladies?" Josh's voice was tentative. "Okay to come inside?"

Alice answered by twisting the antique looking knob and opening the door. Josh flashed a half smile and held up a steaming mug. "I brought you some tea."

Nikki pushed herself up and sat back against the wood headboard as she reached for the cup. "Thank you."

Sitting down on the bed, Josh let her take the drink but kept his palms resting under her hands until the amber water no longer rippled and her fingers stopped jittering. How could she ever have doubted him? She raised the porcelain rim to her lips, letting the steam flower across her face as took a sip. Ah. She'd never take the warmth in a simple cup of tea for granted again.

Josh laid a hand on her knee. "How do you feel?"

She sucked in a breath. "Okay. My fingers are still stiff, and they kind of burn as they're getting warmer but I think I'm fine. When can I go home?"

Alice stepped up to the end of the bed, resting her elbows on the slope of the footboard. "I don't think you should hurry on your way. I think you should rest here for a few hours."

Nikki clutched the handle of her cup. "I can't impose on you guys like this."

Alice pushed herself off her elbows. "Are you kidding me? This is a treat for me. With all the kids out of the house and busy with their own families, it gets awful boring out here. This is the most excitement we've had all year."

Josh chuckled, twisting on the bed to look back at her. "I don't think boring is a word I would ever use to describe George Turner."

Alice pulled her thick, white hair to the side and then started braiding it down her shoulder. "Well, that man has just gone plum mad with all his 'She's trying to poison me' or 'She's digging my grave in the back yard' shenanigans. His poison was a multivitamin, and his 'grave' was a trench for the raised flower bed I'm working on in the back yard. But darn it if I don't still love the senile old coot to pieces. And if it hadn't been for his paranoia this time, we never would've known you'd been here."

Nikki set her cup down on a nightstand next to the bed. She tried to picture her and Josh at that age, but she couldn't quite form the picture. Would they still love each other that many years from now? And why was it so hard for her to imagine? She remembered that she still didn't know what plans her kidnapper had for her and wondered if she couldn't hold on to the portrait of her own happy ending because someone was still trying to take it away.

CHAPTER 18

A BARRAGE OF FOOTSTEPS ON stairs sounded through the open bedroom door and Josh turned in time for Perry to duck under the door frame. He was out of breath and tucked his hand into his side as if rubbing out a side-stitch after a long run. Josh bit his lips to hide a smile.

"She all right?" Perry tilted his head to Nikki.

"I'm fine."

Perry ought to know Nikki didn't need someone to speak for her.

Alice wrapped a hair tie around the end of her braid. "I'll let you all talk in private."

Agent Sterling nearly collided with her as she went through the open door. The agent mumbled an apology and stepped out of the way to let her pass. "My men from Pittsburgh should be pulling up any minute."

Josh wondered why they still needed so much back-up now that Nikki was safe. Unless... they needed help for a search. "You didn't get him, did you?"

Perry's eyes flicked to the floor. "No. But no one does a manhunt better than the US Marshals."

Josh smoothed his hair back with his hand. They hadn't been able to track down Nikki's ex but they had no way of knowing they weren't the only ones chasing him. Nikki threw back the covers.

Perry held up a hand to stop her. "His photo has been circulated. I have all my guys still here from the car crash looking, and the local guys are in on the search too. We'll find him. And with that in mind, we came up here to debrief you, Nikki. Any knowledge you may have of him would be helpful. Maybe we can figure out his next move."

"Everything I knew about him was a lie." Her voice cracked. "I really don't think I will be much help."

Josh reached out a hand and squeezed her knee. "You never know what will be helpful, honey."

"You obviously ran. So when did you realize that he wasn't your brother?" Perry walked over to a reading chair on the other side of the bed.

Nikki reached for her teacup. "Not until this morning. He reached for something. And when he turned around, I saw the skin on his back. It wasn't scarred, but you had told me my brother was badly burned in my parent's car cash. My phone was still in my purse in Josh's wrecked car, so it wasn't like I could call for help. I did the only thing I could think of, I hit him and made a run for it."

Josh raised an eyebrow. "That means the blood we found was his and not yours."

A blush crept up her cheeks, a welcome change from the paleness of cold. "I hit him in the nose." She lifted an arm and tilted her fingers back to show her palm. There was already a purple bruise spreading across the heel of her hand.

"Good for you." Perry winked. "And don't worry about your things. We had some federal guys look at the car but they wouldn't have left town with them. I'll arrange to have them returned to you. Wouldn't want to catch one of your uppercuts."

She smiled. "You don't grow up in state care or have a sheriff's deputy boyfriend without learning some self-defense."

Josh smiled. "He underestimated you."

Nikki chuckled. "Guys do that sometimes."

Man, did he want to lean over and kiss her. If only they were alone. "I don't think he'll make that mistake twice."

"There's something I don't get." Josh turned to see Agent Sterling leaned back against a carved wardrobe. "How did you get free enough to hit him?"

What was he getting at?

"I don't understand what you mean." Evidently, he wasn't making sense to Nikki either.

"He wasn't keeping you captive?"

"No."

Josh's stomach churned. *I see where he's going.*

"Then why didn't you leave before?" The agent pushed his hands into his pocket.

Josh glanced at Nikki as she opened her mouth. Seconds passed but no response came.

Josh heard the wardrobe creak as Agent Sterling shifted his weight. "So, he took you from an accident, leaving Josh behind, and you didn't ask to go back? I mean, you thought this guy was your brother, so you had no reason to think he was going to hurt you if you left, so why not just leave on your own?" There was accusation in his tone.

Nikki glanced at Josh, looking a little bit ashamed. The cup started to shake again in her hand. *Oh, baby, what's going on in your mind?* Whatever her answer, this conversation was going to stay between them.

Josh had to stop this. "I think that's enough for now."

Nikki grabbed his arm. "No. I'll answer. As soon as he took me, I asked to go back and get Josh. I didn't want to leave you. But he told me the Snitch had you watching me, and that was the only reason you were with me to begin with."

Josh felt a knot in his throat. "And you believed him?"

She looked down, resting her tea in her lap. "Well, it wasn't the first time he'd warned me about you and I-I wasn't sure. And then he gave me some water and I got so tired so fast and didn't wake up again until long after dark."

"He probably drugged her." Perry's voice was laced with the resignation that came to officers who had seen too much evil in the world.

It wasn't the first time? What did that mean? "What do you mean it wasn't the first time he warned you about me?"

Nikki let a slow breath stream from her gathered lips. "The night he came to my house. He left me a note before he ran. He taped it to the back of the picture of my family."

Agent Sterling appeared in the periphery. "How did he even get that picture? Was it fake?"

Perry sighed, letting his arms fall on the arms of his chair. "If it wasn't a fake, then maybe he has Rob? He could've taken it from him."

They kept talking but Josh couldn't hear. He stared down at the pattern on the blanket. All the times he'd seen doubt in her since night came rushing back. That was why she'd shied away from his touch. Why she'd put distance between them. She'd been afraid of him. He was ready to give the rest of his life to this woman. To die for her. And it all fell apart because of a note? Had this relationship moved

168

too quickly? Had he rushed her into this engagement? Was she not ready?

"Josh?"

He looked up at her. A tear fell down her cheek. She worked her mouth like she was going to speak but couldn't.

He felt the hurt part of himself push aside the fiancé-in-love version of himself to make room for the sheriff's deputy, former soldier, investigator side of his character. "Have you had contact with him this whole time? Did you know where he was?"

Her eyes went wide. "*No.* I promise. I didn't know where he was and I had no way to contact him. But... "

"But what?" Agent Sterling asked.

Cushion springs dinged as Perry got to his feet. "Let's give them a minute."

"But I still have questions—"

Perry held up his hand. "I'm not asking."

Agent Sterling muttered something under his breath but then turned for the door.

When Josh heard the soft click of the latch, he repeated the agent's question. "But what, Nikki?"

"He came to Apple's. Yesterday when I thought I heard someone out back. It was him. He slipped in and left Anna Duncan a note. She gave it to me. It said he was coming for me and that the people around me were the reason my parents were dead."

That made Anna's attempts to contact him make sense. "And you believed him?"

She sat forward clutching his arm. "I don't now. I promise. I don't."

"But then. Then, you *did* believe him. You thought I was going to hurt you."

Her chin quivered and beautiful blue eyes filled with tears. "I didn't know what to believe."

She doesn't trust me. That's what it came down to. How could he have asked her to marry him if she didn't trust him? He wasn't angry. How could he be? He knew the things she'd gone through. Anyone in her shoes would have learned to doubt people. To start seeing villains everywhere. He should've waited to propose and not rushed into an engagement. He'd just wanted to be with her so much. But when it came down to it, they had only been together a couple of months. He should have earned her trust over time instead of demanding it with a ring. If he had, maybe when she got that note from Kent she would've known the truth. Josh shuddered to think where their relationship would be if he tried to give her more time to grow to trust him. But if he put the brakes on their engagement, he feared it would mean there would be no relationship at all.

***

The questions lasted for hours and all the while she felt Josh was holding back. Like he was only telling her the bare facts. Like how he'd talk to an acquaintance.

Nikki told them everything she remembered about her time with the imposter. Even the mysterious phone call. A development that sent them all reeling with suspicion of who it could be. They were all positing theories and making calls. By the time they left the Turner's, she wondered if the dull ache that had settled in her chest would ever pass.

170

Just like she wondered if this snow would ever stop. She watched the snowflakes flittering in the head lights of the SUV Perry had loaned them to get home. Josh had to be furious with her. Why else had he barely said a word since they left the Turners? His silence caused a pain that went straight down to her marrow. She'd hidden things from him. Hidden things from the man she was going to marry. Why hadn't she just believed in him? Why had it taken so long?

The regret was a sinking ship, and she was trapped inside. It was as if she was back in that creek drowning. Air passed through and out of her lungs, but it choked her like those frigid waters. The worst thing about her mistakes was that, had the tables been turned, Josh wouldn't have made them. Just weeks ago, he'd been in a similar situation, and he'd never doubted her. Not once. Not even when she'd been framed for robbery and dealing illegal drugs and the whole town had thought she was guilty.

But throughout the whole ordeal, Josh had insisted she was innocent to anyone who would listen and fought to prove it to the ones who wouldn't.

And here she'd been given the same opportunity to believe in him and she'd failed. Nikki leaned her forehead against the cool glass window of the door. Tears trickled down her cheeks as she whispered a prayer of forgiveness. After all, she hadn't just doubted Josh, she'd doubted her savior.

Her breath made a halo of fog around her face that pulsed as the air went in and out. Her farmhouse was getting close, and Nikki just wanted to get into her bed and cover her head with a blanket. Josh told her that Lizzy and

Koby were there waiting for them but how could she face them right now?

She glanced at Josh. His arm rested on the top of the steering wheel, and his eyes didn't leave the road. Nikki was going to burst if she didn't stop this. "I thought he was my brother, Josh."

He blinked and turned to her. "What?"

She pulled at the seatbelt strap running across her neck. "I would never have believed someone else if they'd accused you. But I thought he was my brother. That I'd finally found a family. I didn't *want* him to be a liar."

The SUV slowed as they turned onto the gravel driveway to Nikki's farmhouse. "I know."

"Then why are you so mad?"

The car bumped over the snow-covered rocks. "I'm not mad. I just thought you would've believed in... I guess, I just thought that you thought of *me* as your family, too."

Her breath caught. What could she say to that? She twisted the engagement ring—that by some miracle—was still on her finger. *Do I see him that way?* "Me wanting to have a brother. To have a piece of my past that was lost to me doesn't have anything to do with how I feel about you. It doesn't change that."

Josh pulled to a stop in front of her porch. He leaned his head back against his seat as he turned off the engine. "It did though. You thought it was all a lie. That has to mean something."

The keys were still in the ignition. Was he just going to drop her off and leave? It couldn't end this way. *Lord, what do I do?* Her heart pounded. "What are you saying, Josh?"

His throat bobbed as he swallowed. Was he even going to look at her when he did it?

Suddenly, she wanted the conversation to end before something was said that couldn't be taken back.

"I'm saying... maybe we're rushing things. Maybe we should take a step back."

And there it was. How had they gotten here? Just days ago, the world was bliss and now... Now she felt only shock and grief. Heat rolled across her face. She felt the tears coming, but she wasn't about to let him see her cry. "A step back?"

He turned to her and his eyes went wide. Had he not realized the impact his words would have? Did he not see what he had just done?

"I-I didn't say that right. It came out wrong." Josh released his seatbelt and reached across the middle console for her, but she pressed herself back against her door and started feeling for the door handle.

"I think you made yourself perfectly clear." She pushed open her door and jumped out.

She heard his door open. "Nikki, wait just let me explain myself."

Not daring to look back, she jogged up the steps to her front door, feeling him following behind her.

"Nikki, I love y—"

She spun around, almost lunging at him. "Don't you dare say that to me right now."

He flinched, stepping back like he was worried she'd hit him. She pointed a finger at him. "Don't say that."

His face went pale, and his jaw dropped slightly, but he stayed quiet.

Nikki realized how bad her hand—the same had that had broken her attacker's nose—was shaking and dropped it to her side. How had things gotten so bad? She turned back to the door, swung it open, and stepped inside.

Lizzy stood in the entryway, her brow furrowed and her face pinched with concern. "Nikki?"

Nikki clutched her mouth with her hand. There was no more stopping the deluge and tears burst out onto her cheeks. Without a word, she ran up the steps to her room.

CHAPTER 19

THE WEIGHT OF WHAT HE'D done hit Josh as soon as he stepped inside Nikki's house. He felt like an intruder in a place where he'd always felt so at home. They were going to live here after they got married. Were? Was that the word he was going to have to use now? Was their relationship now in the past tense?

Nikki had disappeared upstairs. He thought he'd heard her crying as she fled. Lizzy stood by the staircase, gripping one of the white spindles.

When she turned and glared at him, her jaw clenched. "Let me see. Nikki running upstairs upset after you say something stupid? Hmm… " She tapped her bottom lip. "I think we've been here before, haven't we, Joshie?"

Josh rolled his eyes and pushed the door shut with his back. Like he didn't feel bad enough already.

Crossing her arms, his sister glanced from the stairs and back to him. "Aren't you going to go after her?"

Josh smoothed a hand over his hair. "Last time this happened, you told me not to."

Lizzy scoffed. "Last time, she wasn't your fiancée."

Josh stared down at the floor. What should he say? When nothing came, he just tapped the floor with his foot.

"Josh." She dragged his name out. "She *is* still your fiancée, right?"

Did he even want to know the answer to that question? What would he do if it turned about to be a No? "I don't know."

"Oh, brother." Lizzy groaned. "What did you do?"

The room was getting smaller. The air thinner. He needed to think for a minute. To dissect their conversation and pray that he could find a way to make Nikki understand what it was he'd really meant to say. "I don't need you to make me feel even worse about this." He blew past her, moving down the hall to the kitchen.

The sound of oldies music was playing from an old red radio on the counter and Koby was at the stove, swirling a spoon inside a cast iron kettle. "I'm making an early dinner. Lizzy was gonna do it, but we all know I'm the better cook. And she'll never say it out loud, but she loves my minestrone."

Josh sank down in a kitchen chair.

His friend glanced over his shoulder and his smile faded. "What happened?"

Josh heard footsteps and jumped, hoping to see Nikki, but it was just Lizzy stepping onto the tile.

She leaned over the counter and turned off the radio. "You might as well tell us. We're going to find out anyway. Is it officially over between you two?"

Koby dropped the spoon into the soup and jumped back when the hot contents splashed up at him. He licked a drop off his hand. "You and Nikki are over?"

Josh reached behind him and pulled a dish towel out of one of the drawers and tossed it at Koby. "No." He plopped his elbows up onto the table. "I don't know. I guess it could be." He groaned as hot tears pricked his eyes. *It's like I'm losing Heather all over again.*

Chair legs scraped the tile as Lizzy sat down across from him. "If it's not over, why aren't you up there fixing things? You love her."

Josh smacked a hand on the table. "Of course, I love her. But me rushing up there and begging for things to go back the way they were may not be the best decision."

The gas burner clicked as it went out. Koby covered the kettle with its lid and leaned back against the counter. "What was so bad about the way things were? What's changed?"

Josh drew circles on the tabletop with his fingertip. "The night the man we thought was her brother showed up here, he left Nikki a note warning her not to trust me. She didn't tell me. Then, he visited her at the shop and told her she was in danger and that he was coming for her. Then, when he took her, she didn't run away from him."

Lizzy flicked her long strawberry blonde hair off her shoulder. "She was probably scared."

Josh shook his head. "No. We talked about it. She stayed because she thought he might be right. She doesn't trust me." His voice cracked at those last four words.

Lizzy frowned. "She thought he was her brother. What did you expect?"

"I'm not saying she did anything wrong. She wanted to trust him. I get that. But it scares me that she was so quick to think our relationship was a lie. It makes me wonder if I've rushed her into marrying me. Maybe, I should've waited until I knew she was ready. Until I knew she was absolutely certain that I was the one she wanted to be with."

Josh leaned back in his chair. "The beginning of our relationship was so intense. Someone was stalking her and I believed her when others didn't. We almost died for goodness sakes. And just a few weeks later I propose? I think I asked too much of her too soon. I should've waited. I should've let her have more time to get to know me."

Lizzy looked up at the ceiling and let out an exasperated moan. "And what do you think she learned about you after the conversation you just had?"

Nothing good. He'd made of mess of things. Why hadn't he thought out what he was going to say before opening his mouth?

Lizzy raised an eyebrow and tapped on the table to urge a response, but he didn't have one. "You can't expect two people to be perfect before they get married. People aren't perfect. You could've figured it out together."

Koby cleared his throat. "I don't think that what's he saying. I think he's just worried that if she doesn't trust him, the relationship may not work. Trust is important."

Josh watched his sister's face flush. He'd seen enough fights between Koby and Lizzy to know when one was about to start.

Lizzy turned her gaze to Koby. "It's not about her trusting him. It's about both of them trusting God. No matter how long two people are together, one of them can still make a mistake and destroy everything they've built. But if you both trust God above all else, when the mistakes and bad times come, you can trust that somehow you will get through it." Her fingers clenched into fists on the table. "You don't just give up when something bad happens. You don't just let love end without a fight."

Lizzy may have started talking about his relationship with Nikki but those last few words weren't just for him. He glanced at Koby who had gone pale with his eyes wide.

His mouth worked silently for moment. "Lizzy, is that what you think I did?"

His sister chewed on her bottom lip, holding Koby's gaze for a moment before her lids fell down like shades. All of sudden, she looked tired and spent. "I'm going upstairs to take a nap. Maybe you guys should be somewhere else when we come back down."

***

Nikki scratched Jo's ears as the kitten curled up on the pillow beside her head. Her ring glinted in the light and caught her attention. Should she take it off? *I'll wear it for just a little longer.* Her pillow was still damp from the tears that had fallen before she had drifted off to sleep. She'd missed her own bed every second spent laying on hay last night, and even when she'd heard a door open out in the hall, she'd been too comfortable to get up to investigate.

That couldn't have been Josh, right? He'd have no reason to use one of the spare bedrooms to nap. He should've just gone home. Maybe she should check and see if the SUV Josh had used to bring her home was still parked in the drive. Light was still shining through the windows so she couldn't have been asleep for more than a couple hours. Wanting to listen for voices downstairs, she scooted to the edge of the mattress.

Tiptoeing, she crossed the floor, avoiding the noisy sections of the hardwood that she'd discovered over the past year and cracked open the door. She saw an outline of a figure in the guest bed across the hall but the strawberry blonde hair was not Josh's. It was Lizzy. Of course, she would be staying here. After all, she lived hours away. She wouldn't just pop down for a day.

Nikki felt a surge of affection for Josh's sister. Once again, it looked as if she'd come all the way from Pittsburgh to help her and Josh. What would she say when Nikki told her the engagement was off? If Lizzy had known what was going to happen between Nikki and her brother, would she even have bothered coming?

Nikki pressed the door closed and leaned her forehead against it. Spreading her fingertips over the wood, she let more tears fall onto the floor. Jo pushed her way between her feet and flopped over on her back before letting out a demanding meow. The most vocal of her three growing kittens, Jo was never unwilling to beg for food.

"You hungry, lady?"

Jo rubbed her face into the side of Nikki's foot as she answered with a long yowl. Nikki drew her lips to one side and tapped a finger on the door. Their food was downstairs but Josh could be down there. There was no evidence indicating he had left.

"It might be a bit awkward for me down there, right now."

Jo rolled onto her feet and pawed at the door.

Nikki puffed out a breath. "Fine, but try and be quiet." Just because Josh was there didn't mean she had to talk to him. And if he was down there, she could just tell him to leave.

Her hand dropped to the handle. She cringed when it squeaked as it opened. Jo pranced down the stairs. Nikki pushed the hair out of her face, wiped the remaining tears from her eyes and followed after her.

Voices drifted into the hall as she approached the kitchen. She stopped at the thin, ivory stained console table pushed against the shiplap wall, shrinking behind the burlap shade of a buffet lamp. She recognized the voices as Josh and his best friend, Koby.

"Did either of them come down yet?" Josh asked.

"No," said Koby. "You look a little less crappy now. Did you sleep at all?"

"I got a bit. Nikki's couch is more comfortable than you'd think. Thanks for giving me clothes by the way."

Nikki remembered all the blood and dirt that had stained his uniform. How much had been from been from their wreck? Had he been hurt bad and not bothered to tell her? And why hadn't she thought to ask?

"No problem. A mechanic always keeps a spare set of clothes with him."

Josh snorted. "Could've fooled me. You're covered in oil every time I see you."

Koby snickered. "Hazards of the job."

"Listen man, I'm sorry I started something between you and Lizzy earlier. Just chalk it up to one of the many times I said the wrong thing."

Her heart clenched. Was 'Nikki, will you marry me?' the wrong thing?

She heard a sigh and then Koby said, "Don't worry about it. Things always seem to end like that when we're around each other."

"Why is that?"

Nikki tiptoed a few steps farther until she could see their outlines reflected on the face of her oven door.

Koby scooted closer to the table. "I don't know. Sometimes, I think we think it's easier than getting along. When I feel a taste of what we had, it only serves to remind me of what we lost. I don't know what it is on her end. Maybe I just remind her of our mistakes." He looked down into his crossed hands on the table and cleared his throat. "But you need to worry about you and Nikki, not me and Lizzy. It can't be long until you catch that Kent Marcus guy and the danger will be over. Then, you guys can figure out whatever's come between you."

"Maybe."

Maybe? Nikki stiffened. Then he really had given up on them?

"What are you talking about?" Koby asked.

"I mean, catching him may not mean things are over. What about the Snitch?"

Nikki let out a breath. She moved to just outside the entrance into the kitchen. Her desire to hear better overpowering her dread at what might be said,

Koby sat back, letting his hands slide off the table into his lap. "What about him? He may not have anything to do with this at all. Everything that's happened could be Kent's fault. After all, he was the one stalking her and he was the one with a connection to Vaughn."

Josh shook his head. "That doesn't explain the fire that took the marshal's life."

Nikki recalled the burning SUV. She'd had to get Perry to fill her in on that and many other things while Josh kept his distance.

"That could have just been accident. The guy came down here looking for his witness because he went missing, and his sister lives here so he gave it a shot. And then, he has an accident and the vehicle catches fire."

Nikki stepped into the kitchen. "That wasn't an accident."

Josh jolted in his chair. When he looked at her, she saw something like misery in his face. *Is he miserable because he still loves me and made a mistake wanting to step back or just because he feels guilty for how he ended things?*

She shook her head. "Kent Marcus may have done everything else you say but my brother—my *real* brother—is still out there. I think that he's in danger and I'm going to find him."

CHAPTER 20

THE CHARGE IN THE ROOM seemed to hum. Her eyes were red as if she'd been crying, but he didn't see any other evidence of the tears that, more than likely, he caused.

Koby stood up beside his chair. "I'll uh... give you guys the room." He squeezed Nikki's arm as he passed her on his way out of the room.

She walked over to the far counter and grabbed a clear canister filled with cat food. "I'm just down here to feed the cats."

Lord, give me the right words. "We're going to find your brother."

Nikki popped off the lid and leaned down over a large food bowl on a mat next to the back door. "We?"

The kibbles clinked against the glass dishes as they were poured out, the sound creating the catalyst to the rumble of a tiny stampede as the kittens rushed in. "Of course, we. Nikki, about what I said earlier, I need to explain what I meant."

Nikki lifted her knee and high-stepped out of the pile of furry bodies moving around her feet. "I think you made yourself pretty clear. I forgot I had it on when I got out of the car but you can have the ring back right now, if you want it." She started to twist it off as she juggled with the canister.

Josh jumped to his feet in a panic. Did she actually think he wanted to break things off? "Nikki, I don't want the—"

The sound of the doorbell cut him off. "I have to get that." Nikki replaced the food container on the counter.

Josh reached out and grabbed her arm. "Wait. We need to talk."

She pulled it free and stared down at her feet. "I don't know what else there is to say."

His heart pounded and a ringing sound filled his ears as she padded away.

All he'd meant to do was give her time to know she could count on him. How had one conversation gotten them here? He followed her. They needed to work this out.

Nikki was pulling open the door as her caught up to her. She startled when she saw the visitor through the worn mesh of the screen. "Anna? What are you doing here?"

The hinges creaked as the screen opened. "I heard you were back home, and I need to talk to you and Josh."

At last, he was going to find out what she knew.

"Please come in, then." Nikki took a step back and motioned her inside.

"Thanks. I know this is weird, but it's been eating at me, and I had to track you two down."

Nikki glanced over her shoulder. When she caught Josh's gaze, she averted her eyes and started wringing her hands. "Well, you found us. Why don't we go into the sitting room here and talk?"

Nikki placed a hand on Anna's shoulder and led her under the archway.

Anna was jittery as she sat down in a wing back armchair next to Nikki, her hand shaking as she pushed a lock of blond hair out of her emerald eyes.

Josh sat down on the love seat across from them. "I'm so sorry I didn't get in touch with you. I heard you came by the office looking for me."

Anna waved him off. "It's fine and I'm probably being silly, but I just wasn't going to be able to relax until I talked to you."

Nikki crossed her legs and shifted towards Anna. "No reason to feel silly at all. What's going on?"

Anna twisted her lips, glancing at Josh and then at Nikki. She was hesitating. Nikki raised an eyebrow. What was the hold up?

Anna rubbed her legs with her hands. "It's about what happened at Apple's." She looked at Nikki. "Do you still want me to go on?"

The features of Nikki's face arched with understanding. Josh imagined his own were still crinkled in confusion.

"It's okay," Nikki sighed. "He knows about that man coming to Apple's and giving you a note for me."

Josh swallowed. Just what he needed. Another reminder that his fiancée hadn't thought him worthy of the truth.

Anna looked at him almost as if she was seeking permission. "It's just that I noticed something about him. Something that just seemed weird. It took me awhile to realize it because I only was close to him for a few seconds but I swear he..." She covered her face with her hands and let elbows fall onto her knees. "Ugh. This is going to sound like I've read too many suspense novels but..."

Nikki reached across her armrest and patted her shoulder. "I'm sure it won't. You wouldn't be so convinced that we needed to hear it if it was truly crazy."

Anna puffed out a breath and straightened up, laying her hands primly in her lap. "You're right. It's been bugging me, so I just need to get it out."

"Was it something about how he looked maybe?" Josh tried to get the conversation moving along. The sooner she talked, the sooner she could leave and he could get his fiancée back.

Anna bit her lip. "Actually, it was the way he smelled."

Nikki recoiled. "The way he smelled?"

Josh chuckled. He hadn't meant to. It just popped out.

Anna's cheeks went red. "Yes. He uh... he smelled like Poppy's Popcorn."

Nikki glanced over at him, pressing her lips together to hide a smile.

What did that have to do with anything? "He smelled like popcorn?"

"Not just any popcorn." Anna pointed a finger. "He smelled like Poppy's Popcorn."

Josh was familiar with the popcorn station that Anna's uncle owned at the amusement park. Every summer he'd stock up on it and try to make the kernels last as long as he could after the amusement park closed for the winter

"I know that sounds weird, but I've worked at my uncle's popcorn stand every summer basically since I could walk. No one makes popcorn like he does. I would know that smell anywhere."

That didn't make sense. She had to be mistaken. Kent wouldn't even know about that popcorn stand. He wasn't from around here. *Unless, he's in league with someone who is.* "But the park's closed for the winter. There's no way he would be able to get any of the popcorn."

187

Anna nodded. "Yes, but the booth smells like the popcorn all year. Been like that since Great Grandpa Poppy started the place before opening the bakery and passing it down. It's like the smell comes out of the walls and you can never get it off you. It's like being sprayed by a skunk. It never goes away. Trust me, I know. So, when Lizzy came in to the bakery to buy some snacks for when you guys got back, she said she'd come home because Nikki had been taken by her brother. I remembered the smell and thought, what if he's hiding out there? I know that you're back now, Nikki, but if you're still looking for him, maybe the amusement park would be a good place to check."

Josh leaned forward, mulling it over. It was as good a lead as they had otherwise. "We have to get in there."

Anna reached into the pocket of her jeans. "Well, this key won't get you into the park but it will get you into Uncle Jack's booth."

***

Nikki breathed into her gloved hands, letting the warm air blow back into her face. Thankfully, she'd found an old coat in her basement before they left since the one recovered by the FBI was dirty and covered in hay. Shivering in the snow, she took in the towering wrought iron gates before her and Josh. They were the originals from when the park opened eighty-five years ago with a celebration the likes of which St. Claire had probably never seen again.

She had heard from the folks in town that there were stretches when the park closed because there wasn't enough money, but someone always seemed to come along and get it going again to the delight of the county.

The painted black metal swirled and pitched in Ferris wheel designs big and small. Through the bars, she made out the snow-covered dips and climbs of the two small wooden roller coasters and the park's most popular attraction, the Ferris wheel.

The assorted booths were shuttered and tarped. The lights dark and frosted with ice. How could a place that brought so many people joy in the summer look so sad and haunted in the winter?

"They're here." Josh tapped her arm.

She twisted and saw the sheriff's patrol car heading their way. She looked back at the large lock clasped around thick links of chain woven through the bars. "What if they can't get it open?"

"Laney gave him a key. Her dad was the head of maintenance before he died, and they never gave back the key. You know how small towns are."

The tires crunched the snow as the vehicle slowed to a stop. Nikki saw Brandon Whitaker in the passenger seat and gave him a quick wave.

"Josh, if you think there's a dangerous criminal in there, can I ask why you don't have your marshal friend and that FBI guy here too?" Sheriff Thompson pushed open his door and, with hands gripping the sides of the vehicle, pulled himself out into the wind with a grunt.

Josh nodded to Brandon as he strolled up beside him. "Because I'm grasping at straws here. This may turn into nothing, and I don't want to roll in with the cavalry just to have it turn into a wild goose chase."

Brandon flipped a key ring around his finger. "If someone is hiding out in there, how do you think they got in?"

Josh turned back to the gate. "It wouldn't be too hard to get over this fence if you really wanted too."

Brandon grabbed the lock, letting it rest in his palm as he inserted a large key. "But why hide out here at all? There's no heat or running water."

He had a point but Josh rarely had a hunch that didn't pan out. "Perhaps because he knew no one else would be here?"

The sheriff crossed his arms over his belly. "Hmmm... I suppose that's possible."

When the lock fell loose, Josh started to guide the chain through the bars. "Like I said. It could turn out to be nothing."

Josh let the chain fall into a pile in the snow as Brandon pushed on one side of the gate. The metal scraped against the snow, resisting. The sheriff stepped up beside Brandon and leaned his body weight into the bars. It made a horrible wrenching sound as it opened a few feet. Enough to let them through and to prove know one was getting in here without help. If Kent was hiding here, someone had shown him another way in.

One by one, they squeezed through the gap. The cops formed a line and advanced. Nikki took a place at Josh's side. All was quiet except for three little clicks. Nikki looked at the others and saw that all three of the them had unsnapped the holsters holding their guns. Nikki smiled to herself. Cops sure did think alike.

The snow covered walkway split in two. Brandon veered to the right. "I don't see any prints in the snow so he couldn't have come this way recently but it's the quickest way. You said you thought he was hiding in the popcorn booth, right?" His voice was just a notch above a whisper.

Josh gave a nod as he copied him. The path narrowed. Branches of trees lining the brick pavers reached across for each other. Mists of snow fell from them as they shook in the wind.

The theater design of the popcorn stand stood out even in the snow. They approached the marquee. The large bulbs lining the sign looked dirty by daylight and the various popcorn flavors were still posted on it in big letters like movie titles. The front was locked down with an imposing metal shutter.

Brandon nodded towards the side of the building, and the others fell in behind him. Nikki wasn't sure she understood their silent conversation, but she followed close behind.

As they rounded the corner of the booth, Josh reached into his pocket and pulled out the key Anna had given them. "I've got a key," he whispered.

"I don't think we're going to need it." Brandon replied in a normal voice.

What was it?

Gary and Josh were crowding the door, so Nikki got up on her tiptoes, peering between them. Brandon was right. They wouldn't need the key because the door had already been forced open. And that wasn't all. Nikki sucked in a quick breath. A dark liquid had pooled outside the gap in the door. A liquid that flashed red against the snow. Blood.

CHAPTER 21

JOSH BRUSHED PAST THE STILL damp lining of his coat and pulled his service weapon out of the shoulder holster he'd put on over Koby's T-shirt. He knew without seeing that the others had drawn too. The sheriff flattened himself against the side of the door and motioned for Brandon to take center. Josh looked over his shoulder at Nikki against the wall, but down a little farther, and mouthed the words 'Stay here.' When she nodded, he took his own spot next to the door, mirroring his commander's position.

Josh met Gary's stare, looking for commands. Gary tipped his head towards the building. Josh looked at Brandon standing center of the door, gun drawn, and gave him the go signal.

Brandon raised his boot and kicked the center of the door, sending it swinging fully open.

Josh charged through the opening. "Sheriff's Department! Don't move!" It was dark inside the booth but enough light bled through the metal shutter to make flashlights unnecessary. Josh saw no one. Well, that is, he saw no one but the body.

The victim was crumpled on his side just a few steps inside, blocking the way. Josh stepped up by the head and crouched down. The amount of blood on the ground didn't give him much hope, but he felt for a pulse just to be sure. The man's skin was cold to his touch. He was gone and had been for at least a few hours.

193

A shadow fell over him as Gary stepped up. "Any ID?"

Josh replaced his gun in its holster and started patting the man's pants for a wallet. When he didn't find one, he carefully grabbed the man's shoulder. "Let me get a better look at his face." He lifted the body just enough so they could get a view of his face.

Brandon joined them. "Isn't that—"

"Yeah." Josh cut him off. "It's Kent Marcus. The detective from Pittsburgh who took Nikki and pretended to be her brother and the same man we've been looking for all day."

Gary grabbed his radio from his belt. "I'm going to call this in. We should alert the marshal and FBI as well. Maybe they can get their crime scene techs out here and give this place the federal treatment we can't."

Josh reached into his coat for his cell phone. "I'll call Perry and Agent Sterling right now—"

"Hey! There's someone out here! He's running away!" Nikki's cry came just outside the door.

Josh jumped to his feet and bolted out into the snow.

Nikki was already running back down the path towards the main gate. "He went this way!"

Josh sprinted after her. "Nikki, wait!"

Just ahead of her, a dark haired man in jeans and a heavy coat was fleeing. Fear pushed Josh to move faster. If Nikki beat him to the runner, who knew what could happen. She had no clue who she was chasing. What if he pulled a gun while she was chasing him completely unarmed.

His legs felt like jelly and his chest burned with exertion, but he was able to overtake her, stepping in front of her as he passed. The man was at the gate and sliding through the gap when something jerked him back. He was stuck for some reason. Josh pushed harder, forcing his body to move faster. The man's coat must have gotten caught. This was Josh's chance.

With a grunt, the runner pulled himself free but it was too late. He'd given Josh all the opportunity he needed. Josh squeezed through the gate and dove, tackling the runner to the ground.

The man snarled and struggled underneath him, sending back elbows that were meant for Josh's face. "Don't move." Josh put his full weight on him, pinning him down, as he wrangled the man's hands behind his back. Reaching for the cuffs in his back pocket, Josh told him his rights. After all, he was caught fleeing the scene of a murder.

As the bracelets clicked around the man's wrists, Nikki arrived. "His back!"

Josh looked at her. She was panting and bent over, her hands on her knees. "Josh, look at his back."

Josh glanced down and saw that the man's shirt had ridden up, revealing a badly healed scar across his back.

"What is it?" Brandon and Gary slowed to a stop beside them.

"That's my brother. My *real* brother."

The man stilled beneath Josh at those words and twisted his head in Nikki's direction. His mouth dropped open. "Nicole?"

***

Perry knocked once on the glass of the interrogation room's two-way mirror. "That's definitely Robert Appleton."

Nikki glanced away from Rob's stoic expression. She'd been in his place before—possibly that very chair—when the sheriff's deputies had interrogated her just weeks ago. Had Josh been in this kind of agony, looking in at her while the accusations were thrown? She didn't even really know her brother and certainly didn't know if he was innocent, given her family history, and yet still she hated seeing him as a suspect. This time she was certain it was him. The resemblance to the pictures was obvious.

"Think he's good for the murder?"

Nikki spun around and shot Agent Sterling a frown. Josh glanced at her warily before shrugging. "He *was* caught fleeing the scene. That doesn't exactly make him seem innocent."

Nikki stepped past the men and laid her fingers against the glass. Her eyes were drawn again to the sparkle of her engagement ring. Acid bubbled in the back of her throat at the thought of taking it off. She forced her eyes away from the ring and back to her brother. After her fight with Josh, he might be the only family she had left.

Rob's eyes were locked on the table. His only movement since he was put in there was to rest his head on his hands cuffed to the raised handle-like bar on the tabletop. Just like the one Vaughn had at the prison. Was her brother in the same league as man like that? She searched his features for any hint of emotion, but he gave away nothing. Did his life in hiding make him vicious or just adept at playing life close to the vest?

Perry cleared his throat. "Better get in there and see if we can get anything from him."

"*If* is the right word. Guy's got a good poker face. You coming in with us, deputy?"

Nikki turned, catching Josh's gaze.

"I don't have to go in." His eyes searched hers as if seeking her permission.

Nikki sighed. Whatever had happened between them, Josh was good at his job. If she really wanted all the facts, then she needed Josh to be in that room. "You should go. I trust you to find the truth. Whatever it may be."

"We'll get to the bottom of this." Josh reached out to touch her but then stopped. Instead, he motioned to a black panel on the wall next to the mirror. "If you want to listen in, flip that toggle switch."

"Thank you." She swallowed hard. He didn't have to do that for her.

His looked like he wanted to say something else, but he just turned for the door, following the agents out of the room. Nikki turned on the speakers and steeled herself for whatever painful truths were about to come to light.

Agent Sterling led the way into the room, his lips pressed into a grim line. Rob didn't react to his presence at all.

Perry was next. He stood on the same side of the table as Rob but instead of sitting, he sloughed off his blazer and tossed it over the empty chair next to Rob before leaning back against the wall and pushing his hands into the pockets of his trousers. Rob kept his stare locked on the table until Josh sat down in the chair across from him.

Rob narrowed his gaze at Josh, his pupils bouncing up and down as they studied him. Did he know her and Josh as a couple? Or at least two people who *used* to be a couple.

197

"Do you know who I am?" Josh pointed at himself.

"You're the guy who's always with my sister." And she wanted him to keep being with her.

Agent Sterling leaned forward, crossing his arms on the table. "Then you've been keeping tabs on her."

Rob kept his focus on Josh.

Josh's head tilted to the right. "Whatever plans that dead man at the park had for Nikki, weren't good. I love your sister. So I'm the only one in this room that could understand your actions if you, in fact, did kill him. But if your plans for her are bad as well…"

How could Josh talk about loving her now that things were over? Didn't he realize how painful it would be for her?

"I would never hurt my sister."

Josh pounded his fist on the table. Was he faking this anger? "Then why didn't you announce yourself? If you've been here since you left WITSEC, why not reach out to her?"

Rob rolled his eyes. "Obviously, because someone beat me to the punch."

A sinking feeling in her stomach caused a faintness in her legs.

"Then you know the man whose murder scene you were fleeing." Perry kept his casual pose behind Rob.

Rob shrugged. "He's a recent acquaintance."

Nikki removed a hand from the glass and held it over her roiling stomach.

"Did he work for the Snitch?" asked Agent Sterling.

"Could've been, I guess. But I have a feeling he was only working for himself."

Josh leaned back in his chair. "Why's that?"

Rob chuckled. "Because he's *dead*. Just like all the other people that tried to trick the Snitch."

Perry leaned forward off the wall. "You think the Snitch killed him."

"That'd be my guess."

"Do you know who the Snitch is?"

Rob's eyes fell into his lap. "No. But he knows me."

Agent Sterling knocked on the table. "If you don't know who he is, why would he want to kill you?"

Rob glowered at him. "That's what I've been trying to figure out. All I can think is that he knows something about me I don't. I think he believes that if I see him, I'll know him, so that makes me a danger."

"What makes you think that?" Perry asked.

Rob closed his eyes as a slow breath whistled through his lips. "You marshals have been showing me mugshots my whole life trying to see if I recognize anyone that might be their guy. I didn't remember a single one. For years, I thought I was safe. I mean, the guy was supposed to believe I was dead, right. Then a couple days ago, I went to put some boxes in the attic of my house in Arizona when I saw that my trunk had been opened." He glanced up at the glass like he could see her. "I have this trunk. I've had it since I first went into the program. In it are the only things I still have that belonged to my family."

Nikki's breath caught. The imposter had been telling the truth about someone stealing something that belonged to her parents. How would the fake Rob have known that unless they really were acquaintances? What was her brother mixed up in?

"There's some jewelry of my mom's. Their wedding rings. Some of Nicole's baby clothes and then a sealed envelope of pictures." Rob leaned forward, an intensity emanating from his eyes. Does he see Josh almost as an ally? "You have to understand. That trunk was the only thing connecting me to my family and my real identity. I know every item in it and the order they're stored in. That is... except for the pictures."

He had a whole trunk while she had nothing? What she wouldn't give for a look in that box.

Rob's face reddened, and he looked down at his clenched fists. "Th-Things were hard after my parents died. I was separated from my sister and placed with strangers who knew nothing about me. The marshals gave me the pictures. They thought it would make me feel better, but I never broke the envelope's seal. I was angry and confused. and I didn't want to look at all I had lost. So, I put them away along with everything else."

Her stomach knotted as she figured out where this was going, and the grim look on Perry's face made it seem like he'd figured it out too.

"But when I opened the trunk the other day, the envelope had been opened, and it felt lighter. Someone stole pictures of *my* family, and the only reason I can come up with why is that the Snitch's face is on one of them. Not to mention, the marshals are the only ones who knew my location. What else am I supposed to think other than if one of the marshals knows the Snitch guy enough to steal my pictures, you can bet the Snitch also knows that I'm alive?"

CHAPTER 22

AFTER TAKING A BREAK TO discuss the new developments, Josh still couldn't get past the familiarity in Rob's face. How could he have been so easily fooled by the imposter? The resemblance between real brother and sister was uncanny. They had the same black hair contrasted against alabaster skin. And those eyes. Crystal blue and identical.

As Josh looked through the glass again, there was no doubt in his mind that the man sitting at the interrogation table was Nikki's brother. But what did that mean for her? He might be a murderer. If Rob had killed Kent, Josh could understand the logic behind wanting to protect his sister—if that was actually his intention—but that didn't justify cold blooded murder.

Self-defense might also be understandable as a motive but there had been no signs of a struggle at the scene. Whoever killed the guy, did it execution style. Fast and without mercy. How must Nikki feel about all of this? He wanted to comfort her, but the second he'd returned to the observation room, she'd made an excuse that she needed some air and left. Obviously avoiding him.

Why had it all gone so wrong? One conversation had sent them back to where they started. With a brick wall between them standing strong against Josh's futile attempts to knock it down. Why hadn't he chosen his words better?

Or thought about how they would sound? Josh turned away from the glass and back to the others.

Laney shook her head. "I can't believe you are even suggesting this, marshal. That man is going into lock up."

Perry pursed his lips. "That man is a witness out of WITSEC. That means he's the government's jurisdiction, deputy sheriff. *My* jurisdiction."

Laney pointed a finger in Perry's face. "He just murdered someone in *my* county."

Gary laid a hand on Laney's arm. "Just a minute, Laney. Based on what I saw at the scene, we don't know yet that he killed that man. And if he did, the murder occurred on St. Claire land, which means the city police have a better argument for jurisdiction than even we do."

Laney puffed out a breath. "Sheriff—"

Gary held up a hand. "It's not up for discussion. It's procedure. It will have to be up to Stan to decide if he wants to let the marshals take point."

"I can call him and get him over here." Josh said, knowing Stan Hardwick, the police chief, would come in a second.

Laney twisted around to the door of the viewing room. "I'll call him." She swung open the door. "Maybe I can get him to see common sense." She let the door close behind her with a slam.

Perry gave the sheriff a nod. "Thanks for the assist there."

Gary straightened. "I didn't do it for you. It's the law. If it was up to me, that man would be staying in lockup, and Stan may very well feel the same."

Josh would rather have him at the station where he could keep an eye on him. But if he made a fuss, would the sheriff take him off the case?

Agent Sterling sighed. "It's not like we want to let him get away with murder. I can have my federal crime scene techs check the scene, and if he's guilty, he'll be prosecuted."

Josh rolled his eyes. "Will he be? We all know that Rob's the government's only lead to the Snitch's identity. It may be a weak lead, but it's still a lead. Are you actually trying to tell us that if he is guilty, you guys still won't make certain he ends up back in WITSEC rather than ending up in prison?"

Perry's eyes fell to the floor.

They'd just let a guilty man go free. "I guess that's my answer."

Perry shrugged. "You know how easy it would be for someone like this guy to get to Rob in prison. I'd be surprised if he lasted a day. You're right about my priorities though. I would rather stop an infamous drug dealer and the counterfeiter responsible for countless deaths than prosecute one man for killing the dirty cop that kidnapped your fiancée. I won't apologize for that."

Gary let out a grunt. "I guess we'll see if the city police feel the same."

Agent Sterling narrowed his gaze. "We're the federal government, sheriff. We can have some pretty powerful people insist to your police chief that he let us take over. If we want him, we'll get him."

Gary took a step closer to the agent. "Threats will get you nowhere."

Perry grimaced. "We're not threatening. Luke, just cool it, man."

"What in the world?" Agent Sterling pushed through them towards the window. "What is she doing?"

Josh spun around and his breath caught. Nikki had just walked into the interrogation room. What was she thinking? Josh lunged for the door. No way was he going to let this happen. But Perry stepped in front of him, pushing him back.

"What are you doing?" Josh tried throw him aside but the marshal wrapped his arms around him.

"Let's just see if he tells her anything." Perry grunted as they struggled. "We might get some new info."

Josh growled through his gritted teeth. "This is not happening."

"Josh," Gary said behind him. "Give her a minute. The second anything goes wrong, we'll get her out of there. But let's see what she can do."

Josh panted as he shook himself free. "Fine. I'll give you two minutes. Then, I'm going in."

Perry nodded. "Deal."

Josh spun around to the glass and flipped on the speaker. *Lord, please keep her safe.*

*****

Rob kept the same unimpressed expression he'd given the cops when Nikki opened the door. But when a glance her way revealed someone he clearly hadn't expected, his eyes grew wide and stayed fixed on her as she moved through the room. His mouth fell open. His eyes said he wanted to talk, but he kept silent. He glanced over her shoulder at the glass. What had she been thinking? What reason would he have to talk to her when he knew they must be listening?

However, she didn't care about interrogating him. She just wanted to talk to her brother. Her *real* brother. Nikki felt for the back of the chair unable to keep her eyes off of Rob. It was a bit unnerving seeing parts of herself in someone else, but it also gave her a sense of belonging. She had come from somewhere. A part of her was also a part of someone else.

She sank down into the chair. Her throat went dry and scratchy. Would she even be able to make a sound?

"Did they send you in here to get a confession?" He smirked, although his eyes still looked guarded.

She shook her head. "I-I don't know how much time I have before they come and take me out." She could already imagine Josh rushing down the hall.

Rob raised an eyebrow as he jingled his chains. "What do they think I'll do to you?"

"I'm not sure. I just know they won't like it. Or at least..."

"Or at least, that deputy won't like it."

Nikki pushed her hair behind her ear and then tried rubbing a chill from her arms.

Rob's eyes flicked down. "Are you going to marry him?"

Nikki followed his stare to her engagement ring. She held out her hand, splaying her fingers. The teardrop diamond looked out of place in the room. "I don't know." She wanted to though.

"You look like her, you know?" His voice sounded far away for a moment.

Nikki swallowed. "Like Mom?"

He nodded. "Yeah."

Blood rushed to her face. This was what she'd snuck in for. To get more information about the family she couldn't remember but now that it was right in front of her, she grew terrified. Was not knowing better? Her family could be anyone in her imagination but the truth would always be the truth. What if she didn't like what she found out? She couldn't resist.

"Did you know they were criminals?"

Rob frowned. "They weren't perfect, but they loved us. And they were changing. Looking back, I think they were changing their ways because of us."

Nikki crossed her arms on the table and leaned in. "Part of me wishes I had been with all of you the day of the crash. Maybe we would've been put together."

Rob leaned forward. His fingers just inches from her own. "You wouldn't have made it out alive. It's a miracle I survived."

Miracle. She remembered his terrible scars. It was a miracle, wasn't it? Rob could've died, and if her parents had just changed their plans that day and picked her up, she would be dead too. Something bad had happened to her and to Rob, there was no denying that, but they were still here. And they'd found each other. Even if it happened in a less than ideal way.

"Why did you come here? When you ran from your home in Arizona, you could've gone anywhere. Why here? And how did you find me?"

Rob tilted his head, his brow furrowing as if confused that she hadn't figured it out. "I came for you. I'd asked about you my whole life but the marshals just dismissed me until Neal became my handler. I demanded that he tell me where you were and that you were safe or I would leave the program." Rob's shoulders slumped. "That's when I found out how hard it had been for you. How they'd lost track of you. I demanded they make it right. That's when they made the fake documents about the aunt and the inheritance."

Affection swelled in her chest. "Thank you. That money got me out of an awful situation. It allowed me to get here and open my shop. It's so hard to believe. I'd felt so alone, but someone was looking after me, after all."

Nikki reached out and grabbed his hands. He jolted, looking taken aback by the sudden gesture. His hands twitched, and the cuffs clinked together. Nikki looked down and saw that one of the silver bracelets had fallen free from his wrist. How had that happened. Had he been picking the lock right in front of them?

Nikki gasped and tried to scoot back in her chair, but Rob's hand gripped her forearm.

"Let me go." she pleaded, but he only gripped her tighter.

She tried to stand even though he was holding her down. Her calves knocked into her chair and it clattered to the ground. Rob dove across the table and jerked her into his chest.

"I'm sorry," he whispered as he spun her around. "But if I don't get out of here, I'm dead and maybe you are too." So much for brotherly love.

The door to the interrogation room flung open. When Josh charged in, Nikki fought to run to him, but Rob's arms were like a vice around her. They slid up her arms to her shoulders, and then she felt something cold across her throat. She clawed at it as cold metal links pushed into her skin. She dropped her chin to her chest trying to see. On one side of her neck was Rob's still-cuffed hand, and on the other side, the open cuff was in his fist. He hadn't had time to loosen the second cuff so now he was using it as a weapon.

"Come one step closer and I'll kill her." Her hair flew into her face with his heavy breaths near her ear. Would he really kill her?

Josh stopped on the other side of the fallen chair. She saw panic in his eyes. He held out an arm, stopping Perry from advancing. Nikki saw Agent Sterling and the sheriff behind them, trying to push their way in.

Perry's face was red with rage. "What are you thinking, Rob?"

"Stop right there." Rob's shout sent a shock of pain through her eardrum. "I'm not kidding. I will kill her."

CHAPTER 23

"LISTEN TO HIM." JOSH TWISTED around to the others as they fanned out behind him. "Stop."

The shuffling feet went quiet, but they all kept their guns pointed. Four barrels, including his own, pointed at Rob Appleton. And Nikki, the woman he loved. This room was now a ticking time bomb. One wrong move could crush Josh's world. He had to choose his words wisely. *Lord, a little help here. My own words have only been making things worse lately*

"We're not coming any closer. Just calm down."

Rob's eyes filled with distrust and darted to the others.

The chain across Nikki's neck twisted. She squirmed against it.

"Look, I'm going to put my gun down." Josh's arm drifted towards the table. Praying he wasn't making a huge mistake, he lowered his gun onto the scuffed and smudged steel. Josh stepped forward, making certain his body was between the others' weapons and Nikki.

Rob twisted his lips and looked at him warily. He wanted to look at Nikki to try and reassure her of his love, but he couldn't risk the distraction.

I need him to trust me. "The marshals said you were smart. I guess they were right. When did you find the opportunity to slip the cuffs?"

A hint of smugness appeared around Rob's lips. "As soon as they locked me in there. Had the pick in my mouth since you snatched me up back at the park."

Josh nodded, making himself look impressed. "We underestimated you."

Rob's mouth pressed into a hard line. "Don't do it again."

Josh registered the warning in his tone. He heard the others shift behind him, tensing. "What is you want?"

"I just want to leave. The minute I'm in a car twenty miles down the road, I'll let her go."

Josh reminded himself to step carefully. "If you didn't kill Kent Marcus, why run? The marshals want to put you back in protection."

"Did you not hear what I said about the pictures being stolen from my house? One of *them* has to be a part of this. I'm not safe with them."

Maybe he could get him to blurt something out. "What about Neal Boggs? Is that what you thought about him? That he was in on it? Is that why you killed him?"

Rob's face twisted in fury. "Neal was a good man. I didn't kill him."

That seemed genuine. Josh could feel Nikki's eyes on him, but he kept his stare fixed on her brother. "But you know he's dead?"

A blank look dropped over Rob's eyes like he was recalling something. "Yes. I saw it. He found me hiding out here. I told him about the pictures. About what I suspected. He convinced me he could keep me and my sister safe, and I believed him. He'd done so much for me, I couldn't believe he was lying. We were driving to a safe house when someone in the car behind us started firing on us."

Nikki gasped and her mouth dropped open. "That's what—"

Rob shushed her. A tear fell onto his cheek. "He made me get out of the car and run while he held the guy off. He died giving me a chance."

The same story Kent gave to Nikki, meaning he must've been in the other car. Rob might actually be telling the truth. But then again, he was also threatening to kill the love of his life… "Then don't die now."

Rob squinted at him. "I don't plan on dying now. I plan on getting out of here."

Josh chewed his lip. "The only reason the officers behind me would let you leave with a car is if they believed you were actually going to hurt your sister. But I know that you won't."

That got his attention. Josh sensed the growing panic. "See, they think all that mushy stuff you just said to Nikki in here was a lie, but I know that it wasn't. Why come here—to the very place where you think the person that wants you dead has men—unless it was to protect her?" Josh took a tentative step forward.

Rob backed himself against the wall. "Stay there."

Josh took another step and then another. "You love her. I know you love her because I love her. I recognize your feelings because they are not all that dissimilar from my own. You're not going to hurt her." Josh raised his hand and reached for her. "Now, Rob, I want you to let her go."

Rob's eyes fell closed, and his face twisted into Nikki's hair. When he didn't make a move, Josh started to worry

211

he'd made a mistake and wondered how quickly he could get to his gun, but a moment later, Rob let out a breath that seemed to carry his remaining strength with it. He let his arms drop to his sides, the cuffs clinking as his shoulders slumped in surrender.

Josh reached forward and pulled Nikki into his arms as the others swarmed the defeated man. Nikki turned back, whimpering. "Wait! Don't hurt him."

Josh turned her face back to him and stared into her eyes, begging her to trust him. "It's okay. They won't hurt him. They're just going to have to cuff him again."

"I'm going to put him in a holding cell." Gary led Rob by the arm towards the door.

Josh caught Rob's gaze and mouthed *thank you* as he passed.

"Sheriff," called Sheena's voice from the hall.

Josh looked over his shoulder at her.

"Chief Hardwick is here," she said.

Gary turned to Perry. "Let's see if he'll let you have him after this stunt."

***

"This is not a discussion." Josh slammed the table. "I'm going with them."

Nikki tried to gauge the reactions of the others from her seat beside him at the sheriff department's briefing room table.

"I'm just taking him to a safe house. I'll be fine on my own," Abigail insisted.

Nikki thought the agent looked totally exhausted, but maybe it was just the dark bruises and cuts she'd gotten the other night when Kent Marcus broke into her house.

Perry crossed his hands on the table. "There's no reason why he shouldn't come, too. We're supposed to be collaborating, Abigail."

Abigail gaped at her superior. "I know I haven't been at my best since that guy got the best of me at Ms. Appleton's house. I also know I was involved in a shooting, but I can handle myself, Sir."

Perry thumped the table with the sides of his hands. "It's not about that. Forgetting the fact that we're looking for a leak, I want a local with us at all times. Things didn't have to work out this way. The chief was kind enough to let us take Rob into custody, and I'm not going to repay them by shutting the local law enforcement out of the investigation."

"I still think this is a dumb idea." Across the room, Laney crossed her arms.

Nikki looked down at her hands as she tried to sink into her chair. It had been Josh that had convinced Stan to let the marshals take Rob, and the sheriff and Laney were not happy about it. She knew he had done it for her. Because he didn't want her to have to see her brother behind bars. For now, anyway. However, if he had killed that man, then prison was exactly where he would end up.

Perry ignored the comment. "You and Josh will take the witness to a new designated safe house while Luke and I coordinate with the city police to investigate the murder." Perry turned to the sheriff and Stan. "We already have crime scene techs on route to the popcorn stand, and we are ready to offer any additional assistance you may need."

Stan nodded. "Then let's all get to work."

The chairs crackled and squeaked as everyone got to their feet and started the lazy procession out the door. Nikki stayed back, waiting for Josh to pass her before grabbing his arm. "Hey, can I talk to you a second?"

His eyes were blood shot, no doubt dry from exhaustion. He didn't get any sleep last night and only a short nap today. "What is it?"

Nikki waited until the last person was gone. "It's about what happened in the interrogation room."

Josh raised an eyebrow. "You mean about when he asked if you were going to marry me?"

This was not where she wanted this conversation to go. "Josh—"

"You said *I don't know.*" He looked like he could barely get out the words, swallowing like the words were making him gag.

Was he seriously going to do this now? "What was I supposed to say? You're the one who said we need to take a step back." But then why had he told Rob he loved her?

"Well what I said was not what I meant."

"Then why say it?" What was the truth?

His jaw dropped open, but he hesitated.

"Ugh." Nikki grunted. "There's no time for this. You're going to be leaving, and I need to tell you this."

Josh puffed out a breath and crossed his arms.

Nikki steeled herself. "When Kent was pretending to be my brother, I kept things from you, and I don't want to do that again. Whatever happens between us in the future, I do trust you and I'm not going to hide things. There's something I think you need to know."

"Know what?"

Nikki swallowed. "Before Rob let me go in there, he whispered something in my ear. He said I had to find them and that I've had them all along, and that's why they took me."

His eyes widened like he was surprised she'd told him. "What do you think he meant?"

She shrugged. "I don't know."

Josh stared past her into nowhere. "Okay. I'm going to have the marshals take you home and keep an eye out. Koby and Lizzy will be there too. Once I get Rob settled at the safe house, I'll have one of the other deputies relieve me, and then I'll come find you and we'll figure this out together."

Finally, a bit of hope. "Okay."

"Then..." He lifted her chin with his finger. "We're finally going to have a talk."

CHAPTER 24

JOSH EYED ROB IN THE rearview mirror of the unmarked transport car before steering around another curve in the road. Rob might be a murder suspect, but he was now back under the protection of the marshals, so moving unnoticed was essential.

Nikki's brother looked resigned and beaten. Head leaning carelessly against the headrest with his eyes half closed. Should he ask him about what he'd told Nikki? He couldn't have been any vaguer about the information he had given to her. If Josh confronted him, maybe he'd just come out with an explanation. He probably shouldn't do it in front of the marshal though.

Was Josh giving the guy too much credit? What was he talking about? What did Nikki need to find? Maybe whoever was helping Kent? After all, he hadn't got away from the Turner's farm on his own. And what about the pictures he had of Nikki's family? Whoever stole them from Rob's house had to work for the Snitch, right? Maybe that was the same person helping Kent. And who else could that be but the woman Vaughn said he'd talked to on the phone? And possibly the woman who made the 911 call?

"Take this road up here on the left." Abigail looked up from her phone and gestured across the middle console to a bend coming up in the road.

Josh felt her stewing. Her words were clipped. Maybe she was mad because he was driving, but she was probably just annoyed at his presence altogether, especially given her argument with Perry back at the station.

"You know I had no choice about the driving, right? We took a sheriff's department vehicle. Only someone working for the department is allowed to drive it."

"It's fine." Her tone meant it was in fact not fine.

"Clearly," Josh muttered.

"Just drive."

Josh heard Rob sliding in the back seat. "How much longer until we get there?"

Abigail snorted. "What does it matter to you? We could be in the car for days, and you still wouldn't be able to get out of my cuffs."

"Fool me once." Rob's voice was droll and unaffected.

"Exactly."

How far away *were* they? They'd been driving for over an hour. If he didn't get back to St. Claire soon, Nikki might try to figure out her brother's ridiculous riddle on her own. The woman he loved was smart. There was no doubt she'd figure out the answer, but what if the answer led her right into danger?

"Do you see that gravel turnoff up ahead?"

Josh nodded.

"Take it. Our location is at the end of the drive."

The tires rumbled over the shifting pebbles, sending them bouncing towards the outline of a building. Josh saw the outline of old grain silos in the headlights.

Josh turned off the ignition. He leaned forward, peering out the windshield. "This is your safe house? Since when do the Marshals use silos?"

"We want it safe, not pretty."

217

Josh grunted. Maybe they had rigged one with plumbing and heat. It was inconspicuous. He had to give them that. He pushed open his car door and climbed out, tossing the keys in his coat pocket as he elbowed the door closed. The sound of Abigail's door opening followed. Josh kept his eyes on the scene, inspecting the perimeter for anything that looked out of place, but it was just overgrown trees and field in bad need of a mow. "You want to go in and make sure it's clear before we bring him in?"

"First, I'm going to need you to raise your hands."

Josh registered the sound of a pistol being cocked. He braced himself and slowly turned to find the marshal pointing a gun square at his chest. He scanned the area. Were any accomplices about to step out of the woods?

His eyes flicked towards the car, looking for Rob through the windows. He didn't seem surprised by this development at all. Had he known she was bad news? Josh kicked himself for letting the previous attack on her keep him from seeing her as a suspect. Rob slid across the seat to the doors and slammed his shoulder into them. But his hands were cuffed behind his back, and Josh knew it was a waste of energy.

There was no other option. Josh raised his hands. *I've led Nikki's brother right into a trap.*

"For what it's worth..." Abigail smirked. "I did try to stop you from coming."

***

218

Nikki slurped some soup off her spoon. "This is really good." The atmosphere in her house was tense, and the edge in the air made the hairs on the back of her neck stand up.

The corner of Koby's mouth curled into a half smile. "Thanks."

Nikki's eyes bounced back and forth to where they sat, one on each side of the table. An uncomfortable silence had fallen between Lizzy and Koby that made Nikki want to gulp down the hot soup so she could make a hasty retreat to her room while she waited for Josh to get back.

Lizzy was circling the inside of her bowl with her spoon, creating a slow whirlpool that sent the vegetables round and round.

"Aren't you hungry?" Koby's normal easygoing charm was dimmer than normal and his lids hung heavy over his eyes.

"Not really, I guess." Lizzy murmured something else, still looking at her red vortex. She let the spoon fall against the porcelain edge and sat up straight in her chair. "When did Josh say he would be back?"

Nikki sucked a noodle off her spoon. "He didn't. He just said he would come back when he got Rob situated at the safe house."

Lizzy tipped her head back, looking at the cat clock on the wall. "It's been over two hours. How far away were they taking him?"

Nikki ran her thumb across the inside band of her ring, wishing he'd be back soon too. "They didn't tell me."

Lizzy palmed the table edge and pushed her chair back. "I'm going to call his cell." But just as she got up and reached into her pocket for her cell phone, there was a loud rapping at the kitchen door.

Nikki jolted, dropping her spoon into her bowl with a splat.

"Nikki, let me in."

She knew that voice. "Perry?" She jumped up from her chair and ran to the door.

She barely got the chance to grab the doorknob when he pushed it open. "Is Josh here?" He charged through to the hall, poking his head into the parlor and then the den.

"No." Nikki tucked her hair behind her ears. "Why would he be here? You sent him with Rob and Abigail to the safe house."

Perry wiped sweat off his forehead with the back of his hand.

"What's going on?" Lizzy followed them from the kitchen, stopping at the staircase.

Perry groaned. "We lost contact with Abigail and Josh."

Nikki clamped her hand around Perry's arm. "What?"

Perry's face fell. "When I called Abigail a little bit ago to make sure they were all set up, she didn't answer. After that, I tried Josh, but he didn't answer either. And then, Luke called to say he'd just swung by the place and it was empty."

"If they didn't go there, where did they go?" Lizzy grabbed a spindle.

"If I knew that, I wouldn't be here looking for him."

Nikki's pulse pounded, and she couldn't seem to catch her breath. What was going on? Where were they? Was she about to lose both Josh and her brother? "We have to go find them. We have to go now!"

Perry winced like he'd just been struck. "We don't know where to look."

"Yes, you do." Koby stepped up to Lizzy's side. "Nikki said they took a sheriff's department vehicle. Gary has those vehicles equipped with tracking software. You just have to look for them."

Her heart leapt with hope. They could still be found.

Perry shook his head. "The sheriff tried. Something must be wrong with the tracker or it's been disabled because it's not giving a signal and neither is Josh's phone. We have everyone at our disposal out looking for the car, but we have no idea where they went or what happened to them."

"Do you think Nikki's brother had something to do with their disappearance?" Lizzy's voice was quiet, like she felt guilty for the suggestion. "Maybe he turned the tables on them somehow?"

But I just started to believe in him.

Perry pulled his arm free and trudged into the den and sank down in the sofa, letting his head fall into his hands. "Maybe, I guess, but there's no way to know. I should have pushed Rob harder at the station. I just can't shake the idea that he has the information we need to get a handle on this mess."

Nikki gasped. "What if Rob doesn't have the information we need? What if I have it?"

CHAPTER 25

HE SHOULD'VE DITCHED THE COAT since the damp lining was turning icier by the second. Josh pulled at his tied hands. "You're working with the Snitch?" His voice echoed off the metal walls encasing them and reaching up for the sky.

Abigail kicked dirt at Rob where he lay on his side, his hands also secured behind his back. "What do you think, smart guy?"

Josh scanned the silo for anything that could be useful, but the place was barren and abandoned to nature, lit up only by the moon shining through a rusted-out patch high on the wall. When Rob didn't answer, Josh intervened since he wanted to keep this conversation with her going as long as possible. "Or actually maybe you don't."

Abigail lunged at him.

Kicking his feet into the ground, Josh scooted back up against the wall and away from her wildly waving gun.

"And why do you think that, deputy?" Her lips curled into a snarl.

Josh nodded to Rob in the middle of the floor. "Because if you worked for him, Rob and I would already be dead. He's the one the Snitch wants because he's the only one on the planet who can identify him. The Snitch would want him out of play. Immediately."

Abigail tapped her thigh with the barrel of her gun but said nothing.

Rob erupted in laughter so hard the dirt on the ground clouded around his face.

Abagail stepped towards him and sent a swift kick into Rob's ribs.

Rob grunted in pain, then laughed once again. "I'm sorry." He cleared his throat. "It's just that I finally understand what your goal is. He's right. You don't work for the Snitch at all."

"What are you talking about?" Josh had just been winging it to keep her talking, but was Rob on to something?

Abigail glowered at Josh but that didn't stop Rob from giving an answer. "You're not trying to help the Snitch. You're trying to blackmail him."

Rob rolled onto his back and then pulled himself into a sitting position, moaning because of the pain that was no doubt spreading through his abdomen.

Josh tried to blink away the shock. "Blackmail, huh? That makes for an interesting motive."

Rob shook his head. "Don't you get it? She must have broken into my house and gone through my things. Maybe she heard about my parents' things from Neal or just read about them somewhere in my file. So, they took some pictures—it wouldn't even matter if the Snitch was actually in them—just having my location and possible photo evidence of the Snitch would be enough for him to make you an offer for your silence. But then I took off, throwing a hitch in your perfect plan."

Rob was right. "If Vaughn knew about the Snitch, then Kent would've too. He must've put the word out for you. You must've known each other since you both work out of Pittsburgh and are both in law enforcement. It's totally reasonable that you would've crossed paths before. But if you two were in it together, why is Kent dead?"

"Because he couldn't carry his own weight." She flicked her hair off her shoulder with a snort as she stalked up to Josh. "All he had to do was go to your girlfriend's house and check to see if Rob was hanging around there without being noticed, and he couldn't even do that. You caught him. Although, I will say that his whole 'I'm Rob' scheme lasted a lot longer than I thought it would. But getting caught wasn't the only screw up he had that night." She raised a hand to her head and spun around towards Rob. "When the real Rob showed up and attacked me, Kent's nowhere to be found, and I come to find out he lost the pictures in the woods. Bottom line, he turned out to be dead weight that needed to be cut loose."

Which meant Nikki's brother was not a murderer after all even if he'd been caught at the amusement park. Josh nodded. "However, without the pictures, it sounds like your plans are shot now. Why even bother taking us? Just let us go and maybe the marshals can protect you."

Abigail rolled her eyes and waved her gun towards Rob. "As long as I have him, I have leverage. I may not get the amount of cash that I would've gotten for both the pictures and him, but I'm flexible."

Was she serious? "This is never going to work."

Abigail nodded towards the opening to the outside. "You better hope it does because the meet is happening tonight. Right here. And if I die, so do the two of you."

***

Nikki paced back and forth in her front hallway. "When Rob was holding me hostage, he whispered something in my ear." She stopped and faced the others. "He said I had to find them. And that I had them—whatever they are—all along."

Lizzy groaned. "Okay. What does that mean?"

Nikki rubbed her hands together. "At first, I thought he was talking about a person or persons. But what if he wasn't talking about a *who* but a *what*? I think we are looking for some*thing*, not some*one*."

Perry buried his fists into his sides. "Then we're looking for an object. I'm with you, but where do we look? And what might we be looking for?"

Koby moved over to the staircase and sank down onto the third step. "He said you've had it all along? Could he mean something you have from your childhood?"

Nikki's shoulders sank in despair. "If he does, it's no use. I don't have a single thing from my childhood before my parents died. Everything that wasn't lost in foster care, I left in Pittsburgh when I moved here. Rob is the only one with a trunk of mementos."

The room seemed to deflate. Did they just hit a dead end? Lizzy raised her hands to her face and dug her nails into her scalp.

"Hold up." Perry started gesturing with a finger like he often did when he talked, but no words were coming out. A few moments later, he smiled. "Rob is smart. Smart enough to know that you wouldn't have any kind of mementos like that after being passed around in state care. What if when he said 'You've had them all along,' he meant that you've just had them from the beginning."

Koby leaned back against the stairs, propping himself up with his elbows. "Beginning of what?"

"Since all this started?" Lizzy offered as she leaned against the railing.

Nikki frowned. "Like from back when Vaughn broke into my shop?"

Perry tugged at his bottom lip. "Eh... maybe. That's still a lot of time and places to sift through. He would've wanted you to figure it out, Nikki. I feel like the answer has to be simpler than that."

Nikki let out a yelp and covered her mouth with her fingers. "What if it wasn't Kent who broke in here the other night and turned out the power?" Nikki held out her hands to stifle any protests until she could lay out her whole argument. "Think about it. All this time, we've just been assuming it was him because he was the one that ran from the house earlier when the marshals arrived. But Rob already admitted he'd been following the guy. What if Rob broke into the house with the intention of taking me away but instead ran into Abigail?"

"So, he just beat her up?" Koby's face looked awash with skepticism.

Nikki felt a stab of shame. Abigail was so sweet and was only trying to protect her. Why had he hurt her so much? Why didn't he just turn around and run when she found him? "I can't explain that. I guess we'll have to ask him if we ever get the chance. But I really think, I'm on to something. When we heard the marshals arrive, he decided to run. But what if he got scared of being caught with something he didn't want to lose? He could've easily stashed something down there before taking off into the woods?"

Koby jumped up. "Then what are we waiting for? Let's go down and look."

The narrow wooden steps to the basement sounded like thunder as they raced down them. Nikki pulled the dangling light switch when it smacked her forehead on the way down.

Lizzy pulled her hair back into a bun with a hair tie that was around her wrist. "Where do we start?"

Why had she let it turn into such a mess down here? Plastic tubs and boxes were scattered all over. Random lids and cardboard flaps were lying open from the times she'd come down looking for something she couldn't find upstairs. Or from her attempts to fight off Abigail's attacker with her mystery weapon. Either way, there was no way to tell if anything had been disturbed by Rob because everything looked disturbed. "I don't know."

Koby knocked away a loose lid laying crooked on a plastic container. "If we have to go through this whole place, we're going to be here all night."

What if Rob and Josh didn't have that long? She couldn't give up on them. *Lord, lead us to the answer.*

Perry grabbed her shoulder, turning her to face him. "How long was it from when you heard the marshals and were taken outside?"

"Seconds." She glanced at the few steps up to the storm door. "He would've had to hide it near the storm door."

Nearly tripping over one another, they scrambled over boxes and loose sheets of bubble wrap to get to the doors.

Nikki fell down on her knees in front of the stairs up to the door and started running her hands along the wood of the bottom step.

Her fingertip jabbed the sharp corners of what felt like papers jammed between the step and the vertical board that ran perpendicular to it. "Ouch!" She yelped. "I think I found something." Ignoring the splinters piercing her skin, she clawed at the gap until she got a hold of the papers and pulled. Bent and muddied pictures spilled out onto the floor.

Pictures with the now-familiar faces of her family in them.

The others leaned over her as she spread them out.

Lizzy's hand smacked down on one of the white-framed squares with a thud. "Oh. My. Word."

Nikki leaned closer trying to make out all the faces. When she deciphered the features of a particular smiling visage standing between her mother and father, Nikki's heart stopped.

Koby's face appeared over her shoulder. "Hey, that's—"

"I know." Perry groaned.

Nikki spun around to tell him they need to do something, but he was already pulling his phone from his pocket. After he dialed, Perry held the phone to his ear. "Sheriff Thompson? This is Perry Cole. I need to know where your deputy sheriff is. Right now."

CHAPTER 26

JOSH MIGHT BE FREEZING ON the frigid snow covered ground inside the silo, but he could still see the flaws in this plan of Abigail's and as soon as she saw them, too, she'd panic and they'd be dead.

"The Snitch isn't going to deal with you, marshal. You might as well just kill us and get it over with." Rob's voice came out as a white cloud.

Was he kidding? Didn't Rob realize she could shoot them at any time? If he had some sort of plan, it would be nice if he clued him in.

Abigail glanced down at her watch. Was the other party in this deal-gone-wrong running late? They could only hope for a reprieve.

Abigail stomped her feet as if trying to stamp away the cold. "I'll bite, Rob. Why won't he deal with me?"

Nikki's brother crossed one foot over another. "Because the second he gets here, I'm going to tell him that his secret is out. His identity won't be unknown for much longer."

Abigail made a gagging sound. "Please. You are the only one who has seen him, and you don't even know his name. You're the only risk to this guy's security. The pictures are gone. There is no way anyone will be able to see anything in them after all that rain and snow. And that's assuming someone will even find them. When he sees that I have you, he'll deal."

She was falling apart at the seams. Didn't she realize she'd be coming face-to-face with him soon and, by default, also be able to identify him? If they didn't get out of here, this ended with all of them dead.

"Unless the pictures aren't gone, after all." Rob's voice was careless and easy. So much so that Josh perked up and for a second forgot about his icy fingers.

Abigail stopped her shuffling and pacing. "What did you say?"

"I said the pictures aren't gone."

Abigail waved a finger in the air. "No. Kent told me he lost them."

Rob glanced at Josh like he was wondering if he'd figured it out. "Probably because he was scared to tell you that someone tackled him in the woods two nights ago and took them back. Someone that was following him. Someone like me?"

The marshal's nostrils started to flare, and her shoulders heaved as she breathed in and out.

"He may have been able to hold on to one or two. But the ones you want are somewhere you'll never find."

That was more like it. If the photos were safe, they had a bargaining chip, and he suddenly had an idea exactly what Rob wanted Nikki to find.

Josh smiled as he copied Rob's mocking tone. "I'd say he was right to be scared. Just like you're right to be scared about meeting the Snitch."

"Shut up!" Her mouth snapped closed, and then she turned her focus back to Rob. "Where are they?"

Rob raised an eyebrow but didn't say a word.

Abigail stalked up to him, crouching down in front of where he sat. "Maybe you're right." Her voice was much smoother than it had been just seconds ago. "Maybe the Snitch *will* come in and shoot me after you tell him about the pictures. But what do you think is going to happen to you after I'm dead? What kinds of horrible and painful things do you think he will do to you and your sister to find out where those pictures are? Better to die quickly here with me than agonizingly slow at the hands of a very dangerous man."

Don't trust her. If Rob gave in now, it would all be over. Who was to say the Snitch wouldn't torture them anyway after he found out where the pictures were? There was no advantage to giving in, and if the pictures stayed lost, maybe he'd have no reason to go after Nikki. The killing could stop right here with him and Rob. Should he tell Rob to keep his mouth shut?

The sound of a ringing cell phone kept him from making a decision.

"*Oooo.*" Abigail's face split into a sinister smile as she got to her feet. "This must be him now. I'll put it on speaker so you guys can get a taste of what's coming for you." She tapped the screen and held the phone out in front of her. "You're late."

"That's because I'm not coming," said a voice. A *woman's* voice.

Abigail pulled the phone just millimeters away from her lips. "Who is this? I've never spoken to you before. Who are you?"

"Who else would I be?"

Josh squeezed his eyes shut concentrating on the distorted voice. There was something familiar about it. Could it be the woman from the 911 call?

"Are you the Snitch?" Abigail looked like she might hurl.

"I've always hated that name."

Abigail sank down onto the dirt. "But... "

"Don't sound so surprised, sweetheart," said the Snitch. "You're a woman too."

The woman Vaughn talked to on the phone wasn't calling on behalf of the Snitch. She WAS the Snitch.

Josh watched the marshal's fingers curl around the phone. It looked like she was about to crush it in her hands. "I want my money."

The speaker made another distorted sound as the woman laughed. "You were never going to get any money. Not you or your partner. The only reason I didn't stay around St. Claire and kill you was because I decided to cut my losses and put some distance between me and the federal officers camped out there. I tried and tried, but they wouldn't let me get the brother on his own to take care of the problem."

Josh wracked his brain trying to recall who had battled the hardest to keep Rob. No... It couldn't be.

Abigail smacked the ground with her hand sending up a plume of dust. "Your secret's out. Everyone is going to know who you are."

The voice scoffed. "I saw the writing on the wall. It was bound to happen eventually. That's why I planned for the possibility. But if you still want to get in my good graces and avoid being killed by one of my associates in the near future,

I suggest you shoot Rob and Josh before the police arrive."
The call ended with a click.

She'd called him by his name.

"The police?" Abigail balked. "Why would the police arrive—"

"Drop the gun and put your hands up!"

Josh turned to see Perry charging into the silo with Agent Sterling right behind him.

Abigail let out a low growl and threw the phone to the ground as she swung her gun towards Perry.

A shot cracked, and Josh fell to his side trying to stop the ringing in his ears with his shoulders. Abigail fell back onto the dirt, clutching her side.

Perry replaced the gun in his holster and rushed over to Josh. He had to tell him. Perry tried to pull him forward to free his hands but Josh fought him. "The Snitch. It's Laney."

Perry grinned. "We know. Thanks to your girlfriend."

"Fiancée." Josh struggled to his feet.

Perry pulled a knife from his pocket as Josh turned around. "How did you know where to find us?" Josh held still as the marshal cut the rope.

"We didn't. We thought we were going to find Laney."

Josh rubbed his now-free wrists as Agent Sterling helped Rob to his feet and inspected his cuffed hands.

"Rob didn't kill Kent. Abigail did. And this whole mess was about blackmailing the Snitch. Nikki and her brother just got caught up in it."

Perry nodded. "We'll get him cleared then."

Josh squinted at the marshal. "Why did you think you'd find Laney here?"

"After Nikki found Rob's pictures in her basement and we saw a younger Laney next to the Appletons, I called the sheriff, and he put a trace on her vehicle. It led us here and right into the middle of all this. But turns out it was just a decoy. She'd torn out the tracker and rigged it to a generator so it still sent a signal. It was in the trunk of the department's transport car. Somehow she knew we were on to her and led us somewhere she wasn't. She must've been planning this for a good while."

Josh breathed hot air onto his hands. "I think I have more questions."

Perry winked. "Your fiancée is right outside. Do you really want those answers now?"

Josh's heart fluttered. "Absolutely not." He bolted out into the night, scanning the faces moving about until his eyes found the only one he wanted. She was leaning against the sheriff's patrol car with Lizzy and Koby. Her eyes glittered in the flashing of the emergency lights. Everything seemed to go quiet when he caught her gaze. As if they were the only two in the world. He jogged towards her, passing by uniforms and vehicles like they weren't even there.

She pushed herself off the car and smiled. When he got close enough to touch, she opened her mouth as if to say something, but he silenced her with a kiss and spun her around in his arms. She sank into his kiss as he touched her back, her shoulders, her hair. He'd been so scared he'd never taste her lips or hold her in his arms again.

Finally, she pulled back, her breaths heating his skin. "I can't believe Abigail tried to kill you. Everything's a mess. You don't even know. Josh. The Snitch got away. She's still out there somewhere."

"I don't care." And then he kissed her again. "I'm so sorry for the stupid things I said to you." He cupped her cheeks. "They were thoughtless and misguided, but please know that my intentions in saying them were good. I was just worried that you'd regret it if we got married too soon. I thought everything had to be perfect before we say I do. But nothing is perfect and I know that with God we can handle whatever or whoever comes our way. So, if you'll still have me, I would love to marry you, and I don't care if it happens in an hour or in a year. Just please tell me that you want to marry me, too."

Nikki rose up on her toes and pressed her lips onto his. "Of course, I want to marry you. You're my family."

Josh kissed her back and then hugged her to his chest.

Rob was standing a few yards away, watching them. He shuffled nervously, with his hands shoved in his pockets. He gave Josh a subtle nod.

Josh leaned back and lifted Nikki's chin. "I think he's your family too." Josh glanced at Rob. "Why don't you go say hello?"

Nikki twisted around.

Rob smiled at her and pulled a hand from his pocket, giving her a quick wave.

Nikki chuckled and reached for Josh's hand. She gave it a squeeze and then let it go as she walked towards the oldest and yet newest member of her family. Soon to be *their* family.

ABOUT THE AUTHOR

Allison Pearl is a small-town girl who's lived just about everywhere. She loves books, tea, chocolate, and watching old movies with her husband and black lab. To keep in touch and get updates on new releases follow her Facebook page 'Books by Pearl' at www.facebook.com/allisonnicolepearl/ or follow her on Twitter at @AllisonPearl5 and Instagram at @allisonnicolepearl

Made in the USA
Middletown, DE
16 February 2023